WILDFLOWER

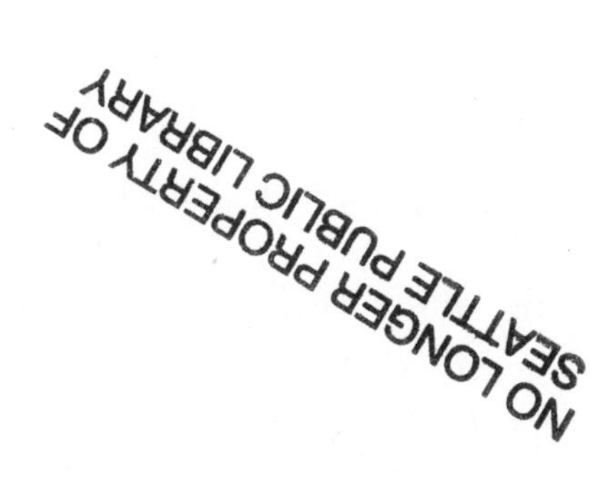

ANNE SCHRAFF

SADDLEBACK
EDUCATIONAL PUBLISHING

A Boy Called Twister
The Fairest
If You Really Loved Me
Like a Broken Doll
One of Us
Outrunning the Darkness
The Quality of Mercy
Shadows of Guilt
To Be a Man
Wildflower

ISBN-13: 978-1-61651-009-1
ISBN-10: 1-61651-009-9
eBook: 978-1-60291-794-1

Printed in Guangzhou, China
0510/05-72-10

15 14 13 12 11   1 2 3 4 5

CHAPTER ONE

"Hold on there, little girl!" Lorenzo Spain called out to his fourteen-year-old daughter, Chelsea. She was coming down the hall, carrying her books. "Chelsea Spain, am I seeing things, or is my daughter going to Marian Anderson Middle School dressed like a Vegas showgirl?"

"Oh Pop!" Chelsea rolled her eyes and groaned.

Monica Spain shouted from the living room. "What's all the hollering about?"

"Monie," Pop replied, "your daughter is about to go to school without most of her clothes on." Pop was shouting even louder now. His son, sixteen-year-old Jaris, was doing some last-minute studying for an

English test. Jaris sighed. He closed his book and looked down the hallway at his sister.

"Chili pepper," Jaris pleaded, "please go put something else on. Don't get Pop all riled up before he has to go to work. There's enough stress for him down at the garage."

"Mom!" Chelsea screamed. "Pop's being impossible again."

Mom came down the hall, and she looked from her husband to her daughter. Monica Spain was a well-regarded fourth grade teacher at the local elementary school. Before she could say a word, her husband demanded, "Where does this little wildflower get these clothes? Monie, you got no sense? You let her dress in trash like this? You help her buy these clothes that aren't fit for decent girls?"

"Lorenzo, calm down," Mom responded. "Trudy Edson took Chelsea shopping with her daughter, Athena. I gave Chelsea a hundred dollars. I had a late faculty meeting. I just couldn't take her there myself."

"Trudy Edson and that daughter of hers!," Pop chided in a scornful voice. "You let those freaks dress our daughter?"

"Lorenzo, Trudy is not a freak," Mom asserted. "She teaches at a high school in the district."

"Ohhh!" Pop said. "That makes it all different. If she's a big shot teacher, then it's okay that she lets Chelsea buy trashy clothes."

Jaris moved alongside Chelsea. "Please, Chelsea, change your clothes," he urged. He hated it when his parents started fighting. The argument always turned into a clash of wills between his tough-minded conservative Pop and his more liberal mother. "Chili pepper, just go in your room and put on something else!"

Chelsea turned around and headed back to her room, stamping her feet all the way. "This is so totally stupid," she whined. "I dress like every other girl at school. I mean, why don't we set up inspection like in the army so I can be checked every day?"

Monica Spain looked at her husband. "You've upset her so much," she said.

"Oh a thousand pardons," Pop replied with mock contrition. "I would never want to upset our daughter when she's goin' out on the street with the whole front of her showing like she's doin' a revue in Vegas or something."

"Lorenzo, just get a hold of yourself," Mom demanded. Lorenzo Spain worked as a mechanic at Jackson's Auto Repair. He hated his job. As a boy, he had dreamed of using his athletic skills to win a scholarship. Then he'd go to college and perhaps be an engineer or some other type of professional. But all his dreams crashed with a sports injury. Now he was often in a dark, bitter mood. He was disappointed by how his life had turned out. Jaris worried about him. Sometimes the darkness seemed to spread over the entire house.

"I got to go down to that stinking garage and work hard all day with Jackson yelling at me," Pop complained. "And all that keeps me going is you and having good kids. If Chelsea is going down the drain, then what am I working for?"

"She's not going down the drain, for goodness sakes!" Mom objected.

Chelsea came back down the hall wearing a modest blue top and jeans. "I hope this satisfies you, Pop," she said. "Maybe I should wear a cape that covers me even more. I mean, wouldn't it be horrible if somebody noticed that I'm a girl?"

"Oh, don't you worry about that, little girl," Pop growled. "Everybody can see you're a girl. Just make sure you look like a nice girl, not like that trashy Athena who looks inappropriate."

"Pop," Chelsea cried, "don't call Athena names. She's my friend. I don't insult your friends!"

"Who are my friends?" Pop asked. "Old Jackson, my boss? He's not my friend. He's my enemy. I don't hang around creepy people like you do, Chelsea. That Trudy Edson wears so much makeup she looks like a clown. I think the next time I see her I'm gonna suggest she sign up for the circus. She can work with Bozo."

"Mom!" Chelsea wailed. "Don't let Pop insult Athena's mom."

"He's not serious, sweetie," Mom said, frowning so much that there were deep lines in her usually smooth brow.

"The devil I'm not," Pop protested, grabbing his truck keys off the wall hook. He went roaring down the driveway, as he always did when he was angry.

Mom looked at Jaris and commented. "Your father really got out of the wrong side of the bed this morning."

Jaris shrugged. He loved both his parents. He didn't want to take sides, though in his heart he usually agreed more with Pop. Mom had a kind of Pollyanna approach to life. Jaris didn't think her view squared with the real world. She didn't know what it was like out there on the streets or even in school. If a girl dressed as if she was asking for attention, she sometimes got too much of the wrong kind of it.

Chelsea usually walked to school with her friend, Inessa Weaver. Inessa was a sweet, quiet girl whom Pop approved of. Now she was at the door, waiting for Chelsea. "Is Chelsea ready?" Inessa asked Mom.

"Yeah, I'm ready," Chelsea bounded out the door and fled down the walk. Jaris overheard her complaining to Inessa. "Pop was absolutely crazy this morning! I had on this really cute top I just got at Lawson's. I was so excited to be wearing it to school. Pop went bananas! He made me take it off and put this dumb thing on that I've worn *forever*."

"That top looks cute on you, Chel," Inessa remarked.

"It's old and it's blah, Chelsea groaned. "*Everybody's* seen it a zillion times. The new top was so fierce."

Jaris didn't have to leave for Tubman High for a few more minutes. He was alone with Mom.

"Jaris," Mom asked, "do you think Chelsea's top was so bad that your father had to throw a fit like that?"

"Well," Jaris replied carefully, "Chelsea is really growing. Last year she was a skinny little girl. This year she's, you know, filled out some. And, well, the top was a little bit . . . uh . . . *hot*."

"I didn't think it was bad," Mom insisted. "I see tops like that on all the young girls."

"Mom," Jaris told his Mom, "uh, the guys at school, even middle school, they're looking at the girls and making cracks. I mean, they hassle the girls with jokes and stuff. Chelsea's only fourteen. Next year she'll be at Tubman. It'd be good if she could, you know, hold off on the really sexy clothes."

"You know, though, Jaris," Mom countered, "your father's problem is that he still sees Chelsea as a child. He thinks she's ten years old and he can boss her around. She's becoming a young lady. She has to be allowed to make her own decisions." Mom disappeared into the bedroom to get ready for school, where she taught.

Jaris didn't have to wonder whom Mom was talking to on the phone when he heard her voice in the bedroom. Whenever Mom had the slightest problem with Pop, she called her mother to talk about the issue.

Mom's mother, Jessie Clymer, was an active, sixty-eight-year-old retired real estate agent. She was in good health and well fixed economically. She had never liked Pop, even before Mom and Pop were married. Sometimes Jaris thought that his grandmother would actually be pleased if the Spains got a divorce. Jaris once heard his grandmother lamenting how many years Mom had already "wasted" on Lorenzo Spain. To grandma, Dad was an obvious loser. It would be a pity, Grandma Clymer had said, if Monica wasted the rest of her life with him. When Jaris had heard this past conversation, he tightened his hands into fists. He felt as though he actually hated his grandmother. She was his only grandmother and she loved Jaris and Chelsea. But the fact that she hated Pop embittered Jaris.

One of Jaris's deepest fears had always been that his parents would split up. It had already happened to his girlfriend, Sereeta Prince, and the divorce tore her apart. Jaris's grandmother was hoping for the one thing Jaris feared more than anything else.

"Oh Mom," Monica Spain was saying, "Lorenzo was like a crazy man this morning. He ripped into poor little Chelsea over a sweet little top she was wearing. It's a cute top, a little bit low-cut, but all the girls are wearing them. Lorenzo made her take it off. Can you imagine?"

Then Mom said other things. "I know, I know. You did say that, Mom. . . . You're right. But I love Lorenzo, Mom. . . . I know . . ."

Jaris gritted his teeth and headed for school. On the way, as he jogged down the street, he thought about Chelsea. A few months ago, she got involved with a jerk from Tubman, a ninth grader named Brandon Yates. Yates was throwing a party. He talked Chelsea into lying to her parents that she was going to a girlfriend's house. Chelsea ended up at the party where there were drugs and liquor. Even B.J. Brady, a drug dealer, was there. Jaris had followed her and dragged her out. He shuddered to think of what might have happened to Chelsea that day if he hadn't done that. Jaris never told his parents about the incident. Chelsea swore she'd never see Brandon Yates again. In return, Jaris promised to keep her secret.

But Chelsea *was* getting bolder. Pop saw it, and Jaris saw it too, even if Mom couldn't. She never would have talked back to Pop before, as she did this morning.

Jaris figured a lot of Chelsea's new attitude came from her friendship with

Athena Edson. Athena was fourteen, going on sixteen. She dressed older than she was, and she dressed the way she wanted. Her parents had thought they might never have a child because they were in their late thirties when they married. When Athena came along, they were delighted and they spoiled her. Athena's mother was a high school teacher, and her father was an insurance agent. They led busy lives. So Athena got to do whatever she wanted, from lip piercing to outrageous clothing. Jaris hated to even think of what Pop would say if Chelsea wanted to get her lips pierced.

As Jaris neared Tubman, his friend, Alonee Lennox, fell in step beside him.

"Wassup Jaris? You look deep in thought," Alonee commented. Oliver Randall was Alonee's boyfriend, but Jaris and Alonee went way back. They were dear friends.

"Oh, Pop had a big blowup with Chelsea this morning 'cause she had on this sort of sexy top. It was low-cut, and Pop freaked," Jaris answered.

Alonee smiled. "My little sister, Lark, is only twelve," she remarked. "My dad is already dreading her becoming a teenager and having to deal with that stuff."

"I wish," Jaris hoped, "Chelsea would hang with Lark and Sami's sister Maya, and Derrick's little sister Kayla. Sometimes she does stuff with them, but she's stuck on this girl, Athena Edson. She's a snippy, spoiled little show-off. I think her being kinda bad is what appeals to Chelsea. She's a bad influence on my sister. What really bothers me, Alonee, is my parents fighting over Chelsea doing stuff. I hate that. Mom's more okay with Chelsea doing her own thing, but Pop, he's the big protective papa bear. Mom thinks Pop is being too hard on Chelsea, and then they argue."

Alonee nodded. "That's hard. My parents are pretty much on the same page with stuff like that. I'd feel bad too if they argued. You always worry that it'll get worse and . . ." Her voice trailed off. She didn't want to use the word they were both thinking about, divorce.

"Poor Sereeta," Jaris said., "She's gone through so much with her folks splitting up. And it's still not good. She likes living with her grandma, but she's all the time trying to find a way to have a mom again." It made Jaris sick to imagine his parents divorced and each of them eventually with someone else. Even now, Mom's principal, Greg Maynard, seemed to like her very much. And Mom liked him. Maynard was divorced. Jaris imagined that he would probably be eager to become the man in Mom's life if Pop wasn't there anymore.

When Jaris got home from school that day, Mom was still working at her elementary school, and Pop was still at Jackson's garage. Jaris was alone in the house until Chelsea came home.

"How's it going, chili pepper?" Jaris asked her.

CHAPTER ONE

"I told everybody yesterday to check out the top I'd be wearing today," Chelsea moaned. "Then they saw me in this old blue thing and started making fun of me. I told them I would look awesome. They're all laughing and saying, 'Awww-some!' when they saw me in this old rag!"

"Mom's got a faculty meeting today, and Pop'll be late at the garage, chili pepper," Jaris responded. "What do you say we walk over to the Ice House for a frozen yogurt, just you and me. They got a new caramel flavor."

Chelsea brightened. "Yeah! Cool! This's been such a nothing day, I need for something good to happen. I'm feelin' so crummy cuz I think I flunked my science quiz! Pop'll have another spasm about that! Athena told me today she doesn't know how I stand Pop. Her dad trusts her about everything. He's not on her case like a parole officer!"

As they walked to the Ice House, Jaris started talking to his little sister. "You know why some fathers are so upset when their girls start growing up and stuff?"

"Why?' Chelsea asked.

"'Cause dads remember being teenagers themselves," Jaris advised. "They remember how they felt about girls in low-cut clothes and stuff. Girl like that comes along, and the guys start drooling. Even if she's a nice girl, and most boys will respect her anyway, some boys will take advantage, you know. Pop doesn't want you to be a target for some sleazy guys."

"I'm not that kind of a girl. That top was okay," Chelsea protested. "I'm plain, and no guys drool over me no matter what I wear. Now Athena is beautiful—"

"Chili pepper," Jaris interrupted, "you're getting awfully pretty. A couple of my friends at Tubman said you're gonna be the cutest freshman in the class next year."

Chelsea giggled. "Oh, that's silly," she chuckled, though it was clear she enjoyed hearing it. "I got zits on my forehead, and my hair is so yucky sometimes, and I'm getting fat too."

"The zits will clear up, your hair looks fine, and you're not fat," Jaris insisted.

"I already weigh a hundred pounds," Chelsea said. "Athena and I are the same height, and she weighs ninety pounds."

"Chelsea, Athena looks too skinny," Jaris told her. "I think she's got anorexia or something. Believe me, chili pepper, you look great."

"There's a boy in my science class—Heston Crawford," Chelsea confided. "He's kind of geeky, but he likes me. I told him yesterday I was buying a magenta top, 'cause he told me once he liked that color. He smiled. He got kinda flustered, but I guess that's because he likes me."

After a while, they were at the Ice House, waiting for their frozen yogurt. Jaris said, "Chelsea, I don't like it when Mom and Pop fight. They were yelling at each other this morning, and then Mom called

Grandma and told her everything. Then she's dissin' Pop like she always does."

"I don't like Grandma," Chelsea declared. "I used to like her when I was little, but now I don't anymore."

Jaris ignored her comment and went on. "I just wish we'd both try to keep things cool around the house, chili pepper, you hear what I'm saying?"

"Oh, so now it's *my* fault?" Chelsea flared up. "I gotta dress like some old lady or something so Pop doesn't freak and start a fight!"

"No," Jaris said, "just don't go overboard."

Several girls from middle school came into the Ice House. Mattie Archer had brought her daughter, Maya, and Alonee's sister Lark, along with two other girls. Jaris noticed they all wore low-cut tops and short-short skirts. One of the girls wore a top that seemed about to fall off her shoulders.

"Hi Lark! Hi Maya!" Chelsea called to them.

When Lark and Maya came over, Jaris remarked, "You're looking good, Maya." Earlier in the year Maya had been hit by gunfire outside a store. The shots were meant for someone else, but she was hit in the leg.

"I'm all good, Jaris," Maya replied with a big grin that reminded Jaris of her big sister, Sami. Sami was one of Jaris's best friends at Tubman High.

"You guys," Chelsea said, "I had this cute top from Lawson's on this morning for school, and it looked just like your tops. But Pop made me take it off. Why does my pop have to be an impossible old grump?"

"I like your pop, Chelsea," Maya told her. "When I got shot and I was stuck in the hospital, not many people came to visit me. But he come all the time, mostly with your Mom. Once he drug Jaris along, another time all of you. He brought me a giant stuffed honey bear, and he talked to me and stuff. He cheered me up a lot, girl. Your pop just scared some boy gonna push you around if you wearin' hot tops, you know?"

"But look at you guys," Chelsea argued. "You guys got short skirts and low-cut tops on."

Maya giggled. "I ain't built yet, Chelsea. And Lark here, she look more like a boy! But you're different. You're what my mama says is 'maturin' fast.' My sister Sami, she says to me I gotta be careful when I fill out. Then I need to wear tees that say like her tees do, 'I pick my own dudes, sucka!' "

Lark frowned. "I don't know if I'll *ever* look like you, Chelsea," she complained.

"Just wait," Maya said, "you just twelve, girl."

Jaris could have thrown his arms around Maya and given her the hug of her life. She was going to turn out just like Sami. All the people lucky enough to have her for a friend ought to count their blessings. If Jaris had tried to explain to Chelsea why she shouldn't wear revealing clothes, he might just as well have tried to fly a lead balloon. From Maya, the advice was perfect.

As the girls drifted off, Jaris felt vindicated. He was enjoying his caramel frozen yogurt when Chelsea spoke up. "Athena is so lucky. She gets to do what she wants. She gets to have her lip pierced, and she can even hang out by herself at the Twenty-Four-Seven store. I don't get to do *anything*!"

CHAPTER TWO

When Jaris and Chelsea got home, they both went to their computers to do homework. Jaris didn't pay much attention to what Chelsea was doing. Then he heard laughter coming from the front yard. Jaris looked out the front window to see Athena and Chelsea talking to two boys. Jaris recognized Heston Crawford as one of the boys. His older brother, Nathan, went to Tubman. Jaris didn't know the other boy. Although they were tall, both boys looked like middle schoolers.

Athena and the boy Jaris didn't know were wrestling on the grass. The boy wasn't being rough, but Jaris didn't like how he was grabbing at Athena. Jaris was afraid that soon Chelsea and Heston would start doing the same thing. Jaris went outside and approached the four teenagers. Athena and the boy got up off the ground immediately. The boy looked nervous at the sight of six-foot one Jaris Spain coming toward him.

"Hi, you guys!" Jaris said in a friendly voice. They all said hi back. Jaris looked at Heston. "Your brother Nathan is getting pretty good on the baseball field. Maybe you'll play baseball too when you get to Tubman."

"Yeah," Heston replied.

Jaris looked at the other boy and asked, "And you are—?"

"Maurice," the boy answered. He had a sullen look on his face. His hands rested on his hips in a hostile stance.

"Maurice, wrestling with a girl is a real bad idea, man," Jaris advised. "You hear what I'm saying? You could hurt her."

Athena gave Jaris a dirty look. "He wasn't hurting me," she objected. "We were having fun until you came along."

"How much you weigh man?" Jaris asked the boy.

"One fifty or something," Maurice replied.

"Athena weighs a lot less than that, dude," Jaris persisted. "You're mismatched. When kids wrestle on teams, weight is considered. So think about that. And have a nice day." Jaris turned to go back in the house. As he got a few yards away, he heard a boyish voice utter a slur. Jaris turned and asked, "*What was that?*"

Heston looked upset, but Maurice looked scared. Jaris walked toward Maurice, who was starting to backpedal.

"I'm not gonna try to teach you manners dude," Jaris said coldly, looking right into Maurice's eyes. "But I'm gonna tell you just once. Get off the sidewalk in front of our house and go home. Because if you don't, then *I am* gonna teach you some manners."

"Let's bail man," Maurice said to Heston. He and Heston took off running.

Athena and Chelsea looked shocked and then angry. "You had no business running those boys off like that," Athena told Jaris.

"I don't like your boyfriend, Athena," Jaris told her. "If that's who that punk, Maurice, is. He has a dirty mouth. I don't like words thrown around like that."

"What he said was no big deal," Athena protested. "You been living underground or something? Music is full of words like that. You stand around any school and you hear stuff like that every coupla minutes. Where you been?" Athena turned to Chelsea, "Come on. Let's hang down at the Twenty-Four-Seven store."

"Yeah," Chelsea agreed, starting to go with Athena.

"Chelsea," Jaris said, "Mom is gonna be home in about twenty minutes. We promised her we'd start dinner, remember? You were gonna do the salad while I fried the chicken. Mom's gonna be beat after that long faculty meeting."

Chelsea shrugged, frustration on her face. "See you tomorrow, Athena," she sighed, following Jaris into the house.

"Jaris," Chelsea complained as she washed her hands to make the salad, "that was so freakin' rude. You embarrassed me in front of my friends."

"I'm sorry, chili pepper," Jaris said as he coated the chicken pieces with crumbs. Mom was usually too busy to do much cooking. They ate frozen dinners unless Pop cooked something, which he did more and more often.

"It's bad enough living with Pop," Chelsea went on, "and him being on my case all the time without you acting like that. I thought you were on my side."

"Oh, I am," Jaris assured her. "I'm way on your side."

"Then you should respect my friends," Chelsea said.

"Is Maurice one of your friends, Chelsea?" Jaris asked as the chicken sizzled in the oil. He threw some powdered potato buds into boiling water and added salt and butter. Then he whipped it all into mashed potatoes.

"No," Chelsea replied. "I don't even know him. He's not Athena's boyfriend either. He's just a guy at school. He's kinda yucky. I don't know whose idea it was to wrestle. I bet you thought me and Heston would wrestle too. But Heston is too nice a guy."

"Mom will sure appreciate that dinner is ready to go on the table, chili pepper," Jaris said.

"I can take care of myself, you know," Chelsea asserted. "You didn't have to come marching out and make a big scene, Jaris. I mean, you acted like you were the marines or something."

Jaris turned, looked at his sister, and spoke to her. "I got bad news for you, chili pepper. I was about two years old when I first saw you. Mom said I could watch you sometimes when she was busy. I'd sit there on my trike, and I'd stare at you. I was scared something would happen to you. When you were two and I was four, I'd take you walking around the yard. I never let go of your hand, Chelsea. It was dumb of me, I know, but I thought you'd get lost and I could never find you again. I've always felt the need to protect you. 'Cause you're my little sister and I love you. It's always going to be that way. I used to need to protect you from getting lost and from dogs, but now I need to protect you from guys like Maurice, and worse."

"But I don't need to be protected," Chelsea cried. "I can take care of my own self. You hear what I'm saying?"

Jaris's face finally turned hard. "Chelsea, do you remember sneaking off to that party with Brandon Yates?"

Chelsea flushed. "You said that was over, that you wouldn't talk about it," she said.

"I never told anybody, Chelsea," he assured her, "just like I said I wouldn't. But we—you and me—we know about it. One of the creeps there was B.J. Brady. He was dealing drugs then. A few months later he murdered a guy and got killed himself in a police chase. You were right in the middle of that, Chelsea. If I hadn't busted in to take you home, who knows what would have happened? I won't tell anybody, 'cause I promised, but I won't ever forget it either, I promise you that too."

"I'd never do anything like that again," Chelsea declared.

"Good," Jaris said. "See that you don't. And when Athena wants you guys to go down to the Twenty-Four-Seven store and hang around in the front as crazy dudes drive by whistling and honking, don't even thing about going. Pretty girls stand around there flirting, and it's dangerous. A girl hopped on a guy's motorcycle last year, and she wasn't heard about or seen for a year. Finally this creep admitted he dumped her body in the bay. He claimed she died from the dope he gave her, but they never found her. Never will probably."

Chelsea grew quiet. She concentrated on chopping the lettuce, adding slivers of carrots and chunks of tomato. "Do we want ranch or Italian dressing?" she asked.

"Just put the salad in the fridge and let Mom and Pop decide," Jaris answered.

Mom came in then. "Oh, I smell chicken! Have you wonderful kids got dinner ready? Oh, I had such a day! That faculty meeting threatened to go on forever!" Mom groaned.

"Yeah, me and Chelsea did it," Jaris replied. "Almost ready to eat."

Mom dumped her briefcase on the couch in the living room and sat down. Jaris laughed. "Mom," Jaris chuckled, "you remind me of Mr. Pippin, our English teacher. Your briefcase looks almost as beat up as his does, and you look pretty tired too."

"Yeah," Mom agreed. "We're talking about budget cuts down at the school. Poor Greg is beside himself. We may have to pink-slip some teachers—good, new teachers who're full of new ideas and enthusiasm! If those people up in the capitol don't get the budget fixed, we'll have no choice."

"That's too bad," Jaris said.

"They do this to us every year," Mom complained. "They can't arrive at a budget until we're on the brink of a catastrophe. We end up pink-slipping teachers. Then usually the district finds the money somewhere—after everybody has almost had a heart attack. Greg and I were going over the résumés of the teachers we may have to let go. One of them is so good at teaching math. We can't bear to lose him. And then there's a young woman with such rapport with the second-graders." Mom leaned back in the sofa and pressed her fingers into her closed eyes. "Oh dear, I hope your father doesn't come roaring home in the mood he was in this morning. I'm not sure I can take his tantrums after a day like today." Mom looked at Chelsea and said, "I'm really sorry about this morning, sweetie."

Jaris felt a little sick. He pictured Mom and Greg Maynard in a professional discussion of important educational matters—smooth, even tempered Greg Maynard. Then he thought of Pop about to come bursting into the house like an untamed beast.

"It's okay, Mom," Chelsea said.

"Let's not talk about anything controversial at dinner," Mom suggested. "Let's just have a peaceful meal. I promised Greg I'd take another look at the records of these four teachers and give him my input tomorrow. Greg is such a dear. He's just feeling so deeply for those teachers we may have to dismiss. They're like family. When we lose teachers who are good and efficient, it's like losing a family member."

Pop came in then, grease on his face, looking even more tired than Mom. "Same old, same old down at that junky garage," Pop complained. "Old beaters keep comin' in. People tryin' to keep them goin'. Old Jackson with his stomach trouble again. I'm telling you, he's giving me stomach trouble just trying to work for him." Pop headed for the bathroom to shower.

"Thank God he's going to clean up," Mom said softly. "Last week twice he didn't, and he sits down to dinner smelling like a mountain of gym socks."

Chelsea laughed. "Pop is like a big old wild bear sometimes," she chuckled.

"I'm just thankful when he gets clean and fresh, and we can have a nice, peaceful dinner," Mom declared in her best long-suffering voice.

When Pop reappeared, he was wearing a crisp white tee shirt and jeans. He was lean and hard, and he didn't weigh an ounce more than he had weighed in high school. He was over six feet tall and a solid one sixty-five. There was no question about it: He was very handsome. Jaris could imagine what he looked like when he courted Mom almost twenty years ago. She always joked that she chose him because he was the handsomest boy around, and you could see it still. Most of the fathers of Jaris's friends had put on considerable weight. Most of them had stomachs sagging over their belts. Not Pop.

Jaris loved and respected his father. He'd always felt that way. As a small boy, Jaris knew of no better place than by his father's side—riding with him in the pickup, going to the fair, fishing at a small lake, watching a football game. He was proud of his father, even when his father was not proud of himself. This morning, while Pop was yelling at Chelsea because of her clothing, Jaris was proud of Pop for caring enough to keep an eye on Chelsea, not just letting it all slide as so many parents did.

"So," Pop asked, "what's new in the world of education, Monie?" There was always a tinge of sarcasm in Pop's voice when he talked about Mom's career. Pop felt being a professional educator made

Mom feel she was a little better than Pop, who didn't finish college. In Pop's mind, she was a teacher married to a "grease monkey," the term he often used to describe himself.

"Oh," Mom answered, "the state budget is past due again, and they're talking about pink-slipping teachers. Some of our talented new teachers are at risk"

"Poor devils," Pop replied, eating a piece of fried chicken. He grinned at Jaris and Chelsea and told them, "This is good!" Then he returned to the subject at hand. "They urge kids to be teachers, like Jaris here. He maybe wants to be a teacher, Then the bozo politicians screw up the darn budget. Kids figure, 'Who needs a shaky job?' "

"Yes," Mom agreed. The tension of the morning had thankfully not carried over.

As they finished dinner, the phone rang. Mom frowned immediately as she began talking to the caller. "No, Trudy, Athena isn't here," Mom said. "As far as I know, she hasn't been here today. Chelsea walked to school with Inessa this morning. Oh my goodness! *She hasn't come home from school yet*?" Mom put the phone aside. "Chelsea, you didn't see Athena after school today, did you?"

Chelsea jumped up. "What's the matter? Is she okay?" she cried.

"She never got home from school," Mom responded.

"Mom," Chelsea said, "she was here this afternoon. I was doing homework and she came with two guys from school. We talked and stuff, and then she said she was going to the Twenty-Four-Seven store."

Mom put the phone to her mouth. "Trudy, wait a minute. I'm going to let you talk to Chelsea."

Chelsea took the phone. "Mrs. Edson," she said, "Athena came over here this afternoon with two guys from school. Heston and Maurice. They're in our classes. They were, all three of them, just talking and stuff, and I went out for a while.

Athena asked me to go with her to the Twenty-Four-Seven store, but my brother said I had to come in and help make dinner. So Athena just left."

Athena's mother asked what time that was, and Chelsea looked at Jaris. "It was . . . Jaris, what time did Athena leave?"

"About five thirty," Jaris replied.

"Five thirty, Mrs. Edson." Chelsea relayed the information. "The boys left earlier. My brother sorta kicked them out. Athena went away alone."

Mom went back on the phone. "Oh Trudy, it's almost seven thirty now. I'm so worried about Athena. . . . Good. You go down to the store. She might just be hanging around there. . . . I know. Lotta kids stand around in front and drink sodas." Mom put the phone down. "That's terrible that a fourteen-year-old girl isn't home yet!"

Pop got a dark look on his face. He spoke to no one in particular. "I see those kids hanging there in front of the store when I'm coming home from work and it's dark already. Young kids, mostly girls. Twelve, thirteen, fourteen. I'm thinking, what kinda parents put up with that? They let their kids run wild."

Pop turned and looked at Chelsea, "Now, little girl. Is that the kind of a kid you want to hang with?" He swung toward his wife—on a roll. "Monie," he declared, "I don't want that Trudy Edson driving Chelsea around anymore for shopping or anything else. She can't be much of a mother to let something like this happen. I don't trust that woman. She hasn't got a clue about the kind of world we're living in. She thinks this is Never Never Land and all the boys are Peter Pan. And those guys who were hanging here at the house. I don't like that either. Cops oughta be asking them some questions."

"I told them to go home," Jaris said quietly.

"Good for you, boy," Pop declared. Then he spoke to Chelsea. "I don't like you outside hanging around with little jerks, Chelsea. Anybody wants to visit with you, they can come on inside when your parents are home." Pop was fuming. All the goodwill from the fried chicken, mashed potatoes, and salad was gone.

"Poor Athena," Chelsea said. "I hope nothing happened to her."

Jaris thought, if he hadn't intervened when Athena wanted Chelsea to go with her to the Twenty-Four-Seven store, maybe they'd both be missing now. Maybe whatever happened to Athena would have happened to Chelsea too. Life didn't often offer you a second chance if you screwed up the first time.

Jaris looked at his sister, at the beautiful child who was turning into a young woman before his eyes. Sometimes she looked ten, and sometimes she looked sixteen. Right now she looked about eight, and tears were shining in her eyes. She looked like she needed to hug her brown teddy bear on her bed.

Pop got up slowly and started clearing the table. He looked at his wife, and his dark, smoldering eyes said it all without his uttering a word: "See?" Pop warned silently. "This is what happens to young girls when their parents don't watch them."

CHAPTER THREE

For a long while, no call came from the Edson family.

Jaris was about to get ready for bed when he heard his sister crying. He went down the hall to her room. He tapped lightly on her half-open door. "Chili pepper? Can I come in?" he asked.

"I guess so," Chelsea replied.

Jaris went in and sat on the edge of Chelsea's bed. "You worrying about Athena, huh?" he asked.

"Yeah," Chelsea spoke softly. "She's not what you think she is, Jaris. She was kinda rude today, but she's not really like that. She acts tough, but she's so softhearted. She's my best friend. Lotta mean girls at school, Jaris, and she's always got my back. You know what I mean? Like sometimes the mean girls gang up on somebody—me sometimes—and Athena is always there on my side. . . . Oh Jaris, you think she's okay? I prayed and everything. What if some creepy guy kidnapped her or something?"

"Chili pepper, does Athena hang around with any special guy at the Twenty-Four-Seven store?" Jaris asked.

"No," Chelsea answered. "She usually just drinks sodas and waves at the cars that pass if they have boys in them. Then the cars slow down, and sometimes the guys whistle. Athena likes the attention. I told her not to do that when it got dark. But, you know, sometimes her mom has faculty or department meetings, and her dad always works late. So she's alone at home and she gets so bored."

"Chelsea, you're right," her big brother assured her. "It's bad to hang out there at night. You never know what kind of a guy is out there looking for trouble. Don't you ever do that, chili pepper, promise?"

"I promise," she said.

The phone rang then and Mom answered it. Both Jaris and Chelsea heard her loud cry. "Oh thank God!"

Jaris and Chelsea rushed into the living room where Mom was on the phone. She put the phone aside and announced, "Athena is all right. She's in the hospital. They just took her there to check everything out, but she's not hurt. Her parents are calling from the ER. They went to the convenience store, but they couldn't find her. They were home when the police called. Somebody found Athena unconscious in the alley behind the store."

"Oh my gosh! What happened?" Chelsea exclaimed.

Mom shook her head. "They're giving Athena tests now, but the main thing is, she looks okay. She'll be overnight in the hospital. If the doctors don't find anything, she'll be discharged in the morning."

Pop stood there listening. “So what’s the story, Monie?” he asked.

“They found Athena passed out in the alley,” Mom replied. “She’s in the hospital right now but she seems okay.”

“Yeah, I heard that. But what happened?” Pop asked.

Mom looked nervous. She was avoiding telling the rest of the story. Finally she spoke. “Somebody gave Athena some liquor, and she passed out apparently.” Mom shook her head sadly.

“Oh, that’s beautiful!” Pop declared. “Real nice. Those are classy people there, letting their kid get drunk and pass out.” He looked at Chelsea with a stern glare. “Lissen up, little girl. Don’t you be hanging with her no more. She’s getting stoned with some no-good friends and sleepin’ it off in the alley.”

“Athena isn’t like that,” Chelsea insisted. “Somebody musta tricked her into drinking that stuff. She’s really a good person. Somebody spiked her soda. She never woulda gotten drunk. She's a good friend. She's helps me out a lot."

"Oh, I can imagine how she'd like to help you out even more, sharing her booze with you," Pop said sarcastically.

"Pop, you're mean!" Chelsea cried.

"No, I care about my kid," Pop responded. "That is something Trudy Edson and her man don't seem much interested in." He turned and headed for bed.

When he was out of earshot, Mom explained what happened to Jaris and Chelsea. "Trudy told me a homeless man was looking for bottles and cans in a trash barrel. He found Athena." A look of horror was on Mom's face.

"Oh wow!" Jaris gasped.

"The homeless man ran into the convenience store," Mom went on. "He told them there was an unconscious girl in the alley and they better call 911. He said he didn't touch her, but he could see her chest moving up and down. So she was still alive. Oh man. Somebody must have given her the liquor and just left her lying there when she passed out. Whoever it was got scared and ran. That is beyond despicable. When you think what could have happened to Athena . . ."

"Maybe she hooked up with those two guys she was with before," Jaris suggested. "Heston and Maurice. Heston seemed okay, but that Maurice was a punk. Maybe he's the one who got her the liquor. They better find out who did this. Anybody who would get a fourteen-year-old girl drunk and then leave her helpless in an alley ought to be in jail."

In the morning, Athena Edson was released from the hospital. She went home with her mother. But she wouldn't be going back to school for another day.

After school, Chelsea asked Jaris if he would drive her over to Athena's house. The Edsons lived in a tract house much like the Spain home. All the homes had been built at about the same time during the building boom. They were nice, middle-class, stucco-and-frame houses. The Edsons lived within walking distance of the Spain house, but it was drizzling.

"Sure, chili pepper," Jaris said. "I've got to study for a history test. So I'll bring my book along to read while you're visiting with Athena."

Jaris had gotten a good deal on an old Honda Civic. It was handy for getting to school in bad weather and for taking Sereeta out too. And it sure beat having to make her ride on the back of his old motorcycle. Now he and Chelsea took the Honda over to the Edson house.

Mr. Edson was at work. But Athena's mother had taken the day off to be with her daughter. When Jaris and Chelsea came in, Athena was sitting in the living room watching TV. She immediately turned the TV off with the remote. "Daytime TV is so stupid," Athena declared.

Chelsea rushed over to give Athena a hug. Jaris found a quiet corner to read his history book. "Oh Athena, I was worried sick," Chelsea told her.

"Yeah, I feel like such an idiot," Athena replied.

Jaris was focusing on the chapter he had to read for Ms. McDowell, his U.S. history teacher. But he overheard snatches of the conversation between his sister and Athena.

"Some guy stopped his car and came over to talk to me," Athena explained. "Some kid. He seemed real nice. He looked real young—like fifteen or something. I guess he had to be older cuz he was driving. We hit it off real good, Chel. We talked about music and stuff. He had this sports drink in a bottle, and he asked me if I ever tasted it. I hadn't . . . I drank some. It tasted real strong, but what do I know? I told him it tasted strong, but he said not to worry and left. And then I got dizzy. I don't remember after that . . . I guess I sort of blacked out."

Athena's mother came and sat on the arm of Athena's chair. "Darling, the boy deceived you. He's a very bad person. I wish you could remember more about him."

"He was really cute," Athena responded. "'But we didn't even trade names."

Trudy Edson said, "You know, Chelsea, some homeless man found Athena in the alley. Some dirty, half crazy homeless man was there looking at poor, unconscious Athena. Just thinking about it gives me the shudders."

"But he called for help," Chelsea said, "so he must've been a good guy."

"That's true," Mrs. Edson agreed. "The police questioned him very thoroughly. They even took him down to the station. They kept him there until they could make sure he wasn't the one who gave Athena the liquor, or that he had hurt her in some other way."

"I didn't even see him," Athena said. "I never would have taken anything from some old homeless man. They scare me just to look at them. Did anybody find out who he was?"

"The police told me his name," Mrs. Edson replied. "It seems he's well-known to them. He's one of those dumpster divers who sleep wherever they can and scavenge for food. His name is Harry Jenkins."

Jaris looked up from his history book. "Harry Jenkins?" he repeated.

"Yes," Mrs. Edson answered. "Do you know him, Jaris?"

"No," Jaris said, "but he's the father of one of my best friends. Chelsea, that's Trevor's dad."

Chelsea's eyes widened, and she said, "Wow! Trevor's dad maybe saved Athena's life!"

"It looks like it," Jaris agreed with a smile. All he had ever heard about Harry Jenkins was bad, and with good reason. He abandoned his wife and four children to fend for themselves when the kids were very young. But now he had done something commendable, and you couldn't take that away from him.

"Mom," Athena asked, "don't you think we should look that guy up and maybe give him a little something?"

"Oh no," Mrs. Edson objected. "I don't want to get mixed up with some dirty homeless man. Once you get involved with them, they're on your back. He'll be expecting more and more help. You never want to get involved with creatures like that." She shuddered again.

Jaris looked at Trudy Edson and thought about what his father said. Pop had said she wore so much makeup she looked like a clown. That was true. But she had an even deeper flaw that made Jaris sick. Harry Jenkins found Athena unconscious and helpless, and he got help for her. He probably knew it was dangerous for him to get involved. He probably knew that the police may suspect him of something. Indeed, he had already been rewarded for his Good Samaritan act by being taken to the police station for a grilling. That must have been terrifying for him. But he did the right thing anyway. Jaris thought that, at least in one way, Harry Jenkins was a better person than Trudy Edson with all her education and charm.

After Athena and Chelsea shared a snack. Mrs. Edson called from the kitchen. “Don’t tire yourself out, Athena. Maybe Chelsea and Jaris should go home now.”

Athena leaned over and whispered something to Chelsea. Then she ran into her bedroom and returned quickly with an envelope. She pressed the envelope into Chelsea’s hand. Athena and Chelsea hugged, and Chelsea left with Jaris.

“Jaris,” Chelsea said when they got outside, “I need a big favor.” It was raining steadily now. Both Chelsea and Jaris had raincoats on.

“Sure chili pepper,” Jaris agreed. “What is it?”

“Athena feels so bad that she didn’t get the chance to thank that poor homeless man who helped her,” Chelsea explained. “She got some money for him and a scribbled a thank-you note and she asked me if we could get it to him. Do you think we could find him, Jaris?”

"Well, we can try," Jaris said, starting up the car. "That was nice of Athena to want to do something for him. It kinda made me sick that her mom didn't feel any obligation to the man. After all, he might saved Athena from something awful. Tell you what, chili pepper, Trevor and his mom have nothing to do with Harry Jenkins. But maybe Trevor could help point us in the right direction. He's told me he sees his father often begging for quarters for booze and cigarettes. So we'll stop off at Trev's place."

When Jaris and Chelsea rang the bell at the Jenkins' house, they heard a "C'mon in!" When they entered, they saw that Trevor's mother had just gotten home from her job at the nursing home. She was half sitting, half lying in the sofa, her shoes off. She looked beat. She was sipping a chocolate nutritional drink. "Hi Jaris, hi Chelsea," Mickey Jenkins called out, managing a smile that wiped some of the lines from her weary face.

Trevor came down the hallway, "Hey, you guys!"

"Hey Trev," Jaris said right away, "we need some help finding your father."

"Oh my Lord in Heaven!" Mickey Jenkins cried out in anguish. "What has the man done now? Hasn't he caused enough grief in this family?"

Chelsea spoke up before Jaris had a chance to explain. "No, no, Mrs. Jenkins. This is something good he did. I got this friend, Athena. And some boy got her drunk and she passed out in an alley. She was lying there helpless, and anything coulda happened to her. Mr. Jenkins come along and found her and called 911 and maybe saved her life. And Athena is okay now."

"Merciful Lord!" Mickey Jenkins cried, rocking back in the sofa. "The man has been on this earth almost fifty years, and finally he has done something praiseworthy!"

"Athena, the girl he helped," Chelsea went on, "she wants to give him a reward. But we don't know where to find him."

"You guys," Trevor suggested, "I'll come in the car with you and point out the places where I see him most often. He has sort of a route, places where people are willing to give him something. We might get lucky."

The three of them drove off in the rain. Heavy clouds darkened the sky, promising more squalls later on.

"I can't believe my old man did the right thing for once," Trevor said in amazement. "He's always getting harassed by the cops. He might've thought he was asking for trouble to have anything to do with an unconscious kid. I mean, the cops probably thought he was the one who got her drunk."

"Yeah," Jaris agreed. "They took him in and grilled him big time."

Trevor shook his head and said, "It kinda took courage to get involved."

They cruised past the pool hall where Harry Jenkins sometimes swept up for a few dollars. They went around the corner to the donut shop where they sometimes gave him day-old donuts. They went down the street to a thrift store with a shed out back where sometimes Harry Jenkins crawled in for a night's sleep.

"Look, there he is," Trevor pointed. "He's been keeping out of the rain in that shed."

"He's all wet. He doesn't have a raincoat," Chelsea noted with pity in her voice.

Jaris was wearing a raincoat. It was a pretty good coat, but it was worn and out of style. He was thinking of getting a new one pretty soon. He thought Harry Jenkins could use a raincoat right now, so he pulled it off. He hesitated for a moment and then stuck a five dollar bill in the raincoat pocket. Chelsea saw the gesture and smiled. She opened the envelope Athena had given her for Jenkins, intending to add five dollars of her own.

"Oh my gosh!" Chelsea gasped. "Athena put fifty dollars in here. Athena has been saving gift money from her grandparents so she can go on that school trip to Washington, D.C. This must be out of that." Chelsea also saw the thank-you note, a simple card with a bluebird on it. The scrawled words read, "Thank you Mr. Jenkins for helping me when I was sick in the alley, Athena."

Jaris parked the Honda Civic and the three of them got out. Maybe Jenkins recognized Trevor, but if he did, there was no sign of it. The father and son never talked or even acknowledged one another when they passed on the street. Trevor wanted things that way, and perhaps his father did too. Trevor was too bitter to speak, his father was too ashamed, and the gulf between them was too great.

Trevor stopped about ten feet from where his father stood. He pulled out a five dollar bill and added it to the envelope. Then he said. "I'll stay back here."

When Jaris and Chelsea drew closer, the man seemed to move back, deeper into the shed. He acted as if he was afraid. Jaris was very tall and muscular. And he looked intimidating if you didn't know him.

"Whataya want?" the man asked in a husky, whiskey-damaged voice.

Chelsea held out the envelope. She took the coat from Jaris's hands and moved a little ahead of him. The man stopped retreating.

"Mr. Jenkins," she explained, "the girl you helped in the alley, she's very grateful. She wants you to have this, and this is from my brother." Chelsea handed him the envelope and the raincoat. The man looked at both of them as if they were deadly snakes.

Harry Jenkins didn't trust these kids. He didn't trust anybody. He thought they must be playing a trick on him. Chelsea held out the envelope and the raincoat. He stared at them and seemed about to make a run for it—out into the rain from the scant shelter of the shed behind the thrift store.

"It's okay, Mr. Jenkins," Chelsea urged softly. "Please take these. We want you to have them."

The sweetness of the girl's voice finally won him over. He came forward. His hands shook. He looked like he had a bad case of the shakes, delirium tremens—the shakes that long-time alcoholics sometimes have. His fingers closed on the envelope, and he grasped the raincoat. He looked in the envelope and gasped. It was more money he had seen together in one place in years. It looked like a fortune to him.

Harry Jenkins turned and hurried off, carrying the raincoat and the envelope. He didn't say a word. He was almost running. Maybe he feared that it *was* some kind of a joke and that they would all laugh and take everything back from him. Sometimes kids played tricks on Harry Jenkins and the other homeless men. They pretended to give them a sandwich in a little foam container. When they opened the container, it was filled with sand, and the kids would laugh.

The man stopped under a streetlight about a hundred yards away, and they saw him put on the raincoat. Then, hunched over, he disappeared into the misty darkness.

CHAPTER FOUR

The three of them walked back to the Civic. Jaris said, "Thanks man, for helping us find him." Trevor said nothing. Trevor's heart was filled with a terrible crushing sadness that this was his father. His father's life had come to this. Yet he felt a strange sense of peace that he had been able to salvage one good memory of Harry Jenkins.

They all went inside the Jenkins's house and Mickey Jenkins looked up. "Did you find him?" she asked.

"Yeah Ma," Trevor answered. "He was in the shed behind the thrift store. He sleeps there a lot."

"What'd he say?" Trevor's mother asked.

"Nothing," Trevor replied. "He didn't say anything, Ma."

Trevor's mother nodded. "But he got it, huh?"

"Yeah Ma," Trevor said. "It was about sixty-five dollars. And Jaris gave him his raincoat."

Mickey Jenkins looked at Jaris and smiled. There was a look of peace on her face. As Jaris and Chelsea left, she smiled faintly and said goodnight, adding, "Thank you, children."

When Jaris and Chelsea got home, Mom told them that their grandmother, Jessie Clymer, had called. She had said she was coming to dinner on Sunday. She had something important to discuss with the whole Spain family.

"This I can hardly wait for," Pop declared. "There are four things that I really look forward to. One is seeing my boss's sour face in the morning. The next is finding termites in the walls. Then there's the sewer backing up. And the fourth is your mother coming to dinner. And I can tell you, the first three I prefer to the fourth."

"Lorenzo," Mom chided in an aggrieved voice. "That is so unkind, especially in front of the children. You know how much my mother loves our family."

"Especially me!" Pop affirmed in mock cheeriness. "From the first moment I met this lady when I was a callow youth, I could feel the warmth of her hatred searing my eyebrows."

"She never hated you," Mom protested.

Jaris tried to focus on the burrito on his plate. Pop had made the burritos for dinner, and they were delicious. Now Jaris bored his gaze into the rich, red salsa, trying to tune out the conversation going on around him. Once he locked eyes with Chelsea, who was also studying her burrito.

"Maybe hatred is the wrong word," Pop suggested. "Loathing. Is that better?'

Mom sighed so deeply that her entire body seemed to shake. "I expect everyone in this family to be courteous and friendly on Sunday when Mother comes," she demanded in a stern voice.

"Oh man!" Pop whined in an unusually high-pitched voice. "The kids and I were planning to burn her at the stake. You mean we can't do that? Chelsea's already cut up the little sticks to start the fire, and Jaris brought the coals. Right Jaris?"

"Uh," Jaris replied desperate to change the subject. "It sure is great that Athena got home safely. She's doing good too. She's coming back to school tomorrow, right, chili pepper?"

"Yes," Chelsea said. "She's really anxious to be back at school. She's bored out of her mind at home."

Pop was now in a thoroughly bad mood. Anticipating his mother-in-law's visit was enough to drive every benign thought from his mind. The weekend, so precious to him as a respite from his hated work, was destroyed. "If Athena is bored around the house," he suggested glumly, "maybe she could get some literature on the perils of alcohol. That ought to be good, Chelsea. Or maybe she and her mom could read a bedtime story. It could be about how parents ought to keep an eye on their kids when the moon is shining in the sky."

Jaris finished his dinner and fled to his room to go on the Internet. Chelsea quickly followed him.

"I wish she wasn't coming," Chelsea confided to her brother.

"You and me both," Jaris agreed. "By the way, do you think Athena really doesn't know the guy who gave her the liquor? Or is she covering up for somebody?"

Chelsea shrugged. "I'm not sure, Jare. I know it wasn't Heston. He's too nice a guy. But that Maurice, I don't know him."

"I'd sure like a piece of the creep who did that to a fourteen-year-old kid," Jaris said. "Keep your ears open, chili pepper, in case you hear anything."

Jaris intended to keep his ears open the next day at Tubman High. Maybe he could pick up something from the conversations around the lunch tables in the freshman area. Athena said the guy who gave her the liquor looked about fifteen. That would make him a Tubman freshman, if she was right. Jaris wasn't close to anybody at Tubman with a freshman brother or sister. So he wasn't sure he could pick up anything.

On Sunday, at eleven thirty, Jessie Clymer pulled into the Spain driveway in her sporty red convertible. At sixty-eight, with fine skin and classic features as well as an erect posture for her slim frame, she looked years younger. Even though Jaris did not want to see her, he had to admit she was a fine looking older woman.

Grandma Jessie hugged and kissed her daughter on both cheeks. Then she kissed a reluctant Chelsea and an even more reluctant Jaris. She shook hands with Pop. She looked at him as if he were a marginally friendly ape who had just come out of the jungle and who may be a bit dangerous if approached incorrectly. Pop looked at her as if she were a beautiful but deadly coral snake, making its way out of the sofa cushions with the intent of fatally biting him.

A wonderful dinner was on the table, unlike what usually appeared on the Spain table, even on Sundays, except when Pop was cooking. This time, Jaris's parents agreed that Pop would not do the cooking. Mom was afraid his soul food would distress her mother. And Pop did not feel inclined to do his mother-in-law any favors.

Mom relied on Sami Archer's mother, Mattie, and Alonee's mother, Dawna, who produced a beef and artichoke fettuccine with roast beef, marinated artichoke hearts, and grated Parmesan cheese. A honey-lime fruit salad, gorgeous with melons and strawberries, completed the meal.

"Well," Grandma Jessie exclaimed with delight, "this looks wonderful! Monica, you have outdone yourself!"

Pop sat there mouthing the words while Grandmas Jessie wasn't looking: "No dinner out of cardboard boxes today, Granny."

Dawna and Mattie had long ago escaped the scene of their accomplishments.

"Well, how are you doing in school, Jaris?" Grandma Jessie asked as she nibbled on the artichoke heart. She had let Mom know how partial she was to artichokes.

"Great, really good," Jaris replied. "Everything is going great."

"My," Grandma Jessie commented, "two 'greats' in one sentence. Let's hope we do not 'protest too much'!" She laughed with a sound like breaking glass.

Then Grandma turned her attention to Chelsea. Chelsea felt like a poor butterfly pinned to a frame. She always hated to see a butterfly skewered and unable to flee. "I understand you've become quite the little fashion plate," Grandma Jessie remarked, "wearing all the newest clothes, dear. The young girls dress quite differently today than in *my* day. Goodness, we thought it daring if the bottoms of our knees showed. Now girls are wearing skirts that barely cover their derrières!"

"In *your* day," Jaris thought bitterly, even though he knew that wasn't true, "girls wore hoop skirts and bonnets." As he'd done so many times before, Jaris fervently wished again that Mom wouldn't share every detail of their family life with her mother. Grandma Jessie knew all about Chelsea and Pop fighting over her clothing even though it was none of her business. Jaris thought that what happened in the Spain house should stay there.

"I just wear regular clothes like all the kids," Chelsea replied glumly. She stared at the artichoke hearts as if they were worms.

"And what about your friends, sweetie?" Grandma asked in a voice both syrupy and sharp. "I understand one of your little friends got into serious trouble after a drinking bout. I believe her name is Athena?"

Chelsea glanced at her mother. Jaris could see the rage in his sister's eyes, and he thought it was deserved. Chelsea was thinking, "Oh no, Mom! Did you have to even tell her about *that*? Is nothing private around here? Oh Mom, how could you?"

Mom just sat there eating a strawberry. She had always said she was very close to her mother, and even as a teenager she told her mother everything. She couldn't change that pattern now, even though she was nearing forty. Whenever anything happened in her life, Grandma was the first to know.

"Athena was tricked into drinking some liquor and she got sick is all," Chelsea answered bitterly. "But she's fine now. It was no big deal."

"Oh, I understand it was a bit more than that, sweetheart," Grandma stated sternly. "The poor girl was lying unconscious in an alley. And any evil person coming along had her at his mercy. Fortunately, some wretched homeless man called the police, and the child was taken to the hospital. How distressed you must have been,

Chelsea, to see the dangerous streets almost claim the life of your little friend."

Chelsea looked at her mother again with anger. "Mom," her eyes silently demanded, "did you have to share every ugly detail? How could you?" To Chelsea, Grandma began to resemble the big bad wolf in the "Little Red Riding Hood" story. Her perfect dentures gleamed with malice from her red-rimmed mouth.

"It is, unfortunately, the neighborhood," Grandma Jessie declared. "The children who live here are caught up in the chaos of this place. Drinking, drugs, the gangs running wild. No wonder this poor Athena fell victim. It wasn't the child's fault. She fell victim to the evil around her."

Pop had remained silent until now, but Grandma Jessie's agenda was beginning to emerge. Pop had been dutifully eating his artichoke hearts, which he hated, and the roast beef, which didn't taste like roast beef that he was used to. Now it was time to join the conversation. He avoided looking directly at his mother-in-law for fear the distaste for her in his face might be too apparent. He said, "This is a good neighborhood, Jessie. Lot of good people helping one another out. We couldn't ask for better neighbors, better friends. Jaris and Chelsea have good friends, and they're doing fine in school. We're pretty happy here."

"Ah, easy to say, Lorenzo," Grandma Jessie countered, "but not quite accurate. Look at that murderer who was dealing drugs in this neighborhood just a few months ago. Look on the Internet for the crime statistics of this neighborhood. And the dreadful denizens of the streets staggering around looking for money. On my way over here I saw some of those pitiable creatures wandering about. I thought, 'How unwholesome for the young people.'" Grandma Jessie shook her head. "And the way the streets are named for Indian tribes . . . *what* is that all about?"

"We like our street names, Jessie," Pop stated. "It's good to have the streets named for the Native Americans who were here before us. Better than naming streets after nuts . . . Almond, Walnut, Acorn."

Chelsea giggled a little, encouraging Pop to go further. "See, Jessie, lot of streets named for old white guys, but our great nation is made up of lotta different people. And it's time we recognize the first Americans who got run off the land, right?" There was a wild look on Pop's face. He changed from being sullen and silent to deliberately provocative. Mom shot nervous glances at him, wondering how far he would go.

"What a quaint perspective," Grandma Jessie replied, in a stately tone. "Well, I believe it's time now to get to the heart of the matter."

"No!" Jaris thought, "Just go home, Grandma. You've had the artichoke hearts that Mattie and Dawna made because you said you liked them. We've been pleasant up to now. Please just go home now and leave us in peace."

"Jaris," Grandma Jessie started, "probably remembers the lovely dinner he and I had on the coast, just the two of us, that heavenly shrimp salad. Wasn't it wonderful, Jaris?"

"I remember," Jaris thought. "The shrimp tasted funny and being with you, Grandma, was so stressful that I almost barfed." Out loud he replied, "Uh-huh."

"Well," Grandma Jessie went on, speaking to the table at large, "at that time I offered Jaris the chance to do his senior year at a wonderful private school in Santa Barbara. But he declined. He said his funny little friends at Tubman High School were more important than his education. Well, so be it. But right now I am deeply concerned about Chelsea's future. Chelsea, you are completing your eighth grade at that woefully inadequate Marian Anderson Middle School. What a crime to name such a miserable place after such a marvelous woman of song as Marian Anderson. Now the crime-ridden environs of Tubman High are about to claim you, child. And I have come today with a plan to rescue you. This splendid high school in Santa Barbara has a beautiful dorm where you could live, and I would gladly pay all the expenses."

A frantic look came to Chelsea's face and she yelled, "No! I don't want to go to some freakin' boarding school in Santa Barbara. I don't want to leave here. That's the craziest thing I ever heard of. I love it here with Mom and Pop and Jaris, and I'm looking forward to going to Tubman next year. This is the most stupid—"

"Chelsea, calm down," Mom implored.

"Grandma, forget it!" Chelsea continued in a high-pitched voice. "Why would I want to go to some stupid school in Santa Barbara and live in some old dorm? I love my bedroom and my family and all my friends right here! Where did you get such a stupid idea?"

"It is not a stupid idea," Grandma responded in a shaken voice. She looked almost distraught at Chelsea's fury. When she made a similar offer to Jaris, he at least was fairly civil. This child was out of control. "This school is one of the most respected in the state. And you would be living and learning with the best and the brightest children of—"

"*No!*" Chelsea cut into her words. Chelsea jumped up from her chair, knocking over what remained of her artichoke hearts and almost spilling them into Grandma's lap. Chelsea yelled at her grandmother again. "I don't want to hear about your freakin' school in Santa Barbara! Why are you coming here to meddle in our lives anyway? Why don't you leave us alone?"

"Chelsea," Mom cried as she tried to scoop up the artichokes from the floor. "Stop it! Stop it this minute."

"I won't stop it," Chelsea insisted. "She's got no right to come here and stick her nose into my family's business. Why do you just want to make trouble, Grandma? You make me sick! You really make me sick!"

"Ohhh!" Grandma Jessie moaned. "This is far worse than I expected. The poor child is out of control. She's like a wild thing." Grandma Jessie turned toward her daughter, who was halfway under the table retrieving an artichoke heart. Bent over to see Mom under the table, Grandma asked, "Is she seeing a counselor for these anger issues, Monica? Please tell me that she is."

"Ohhhh-kayyy!" Pop boomed. "I think dinner is over now, and we can all go our separate ways. It was really a delight having you here today, Jessie. Like always, you have added to the tranquility and happiness of this family. That is thanks largely to your dear daughter, who shares with you the most intimate details of our private lives." Pop's voice dripped with sarcasm.

"Lorenzo!" Mom groaned.

Pop walked to the closet where Grandma Jessie's light, fashionable little jacket hung. "Here, you may don your jacket now, dear lady, and be on your way," Pop said. "We have shared artichoke hearts together, and someday we will dine again. But I pray not soon."

Grandma walked to the closet and retrieved her jacket, putting it on. Her face was a study in restrained rage. "I do not think I have ever been so insulted," she announced.

"Mom, I am *so* sorry," her daughter whimpered.

"Good day to you," Pop said as Grandma Jessie almost jogged out the door toward her car in her haste to leave the Spain house. Pop flung the door shut after her, causing the house to tremble.

Then Pop strode over to Chelsea who sat slumped at the kitchen table. He grasped Chelsea's hands and pulled her to her feet. Then he began whirling her around the floor in a dance as he sang in a lusty voice.

> The witch is gone, the witch is gone,
> Hurrah, hurrah, the wicked witch is
> gone away!

Chelsea had been near tears, but now she began to laugh as she and her father spun around the floor. Jaris watched the spectacle, hiding his own glee behind a serious and thoughtful look. Occasionally he glanced at his stunned mother. Then he looked quickly away, grinning behind his hand.

"I am humiliated," Mom declared as the red convertible vanished down the street. "I am mortified."

Pop turned to scraping the remains of the meal into the garbage disposal. "No more artichoke hearts for this family, thank you very much," he announced.

"Lorenzo, you almost threw my mother out of this house," Mom cried.

"Nah," Pop objected, "I didn't do that. I think she was ready to leave, don't you think? I mean, hey, she'd accomplished what she came for. She got everybody upset. In her ballpark that's a home run. You hear what I'm saying?"

Mom turned to Chelsea. "What got into you?" she demanded.

"I was just so scared," Chelsea responded. "It was like she wanted to send me away. Like Sereeta Prince's mean old stepfather and her mom, they wanted to get rid of Sereeta. I was scared she'd talk you guys into sending me away. I love you, Mom and Pop and Jaris, and . . . how could anybody think I didn't want to live here anymore?"

Tears ran down Chelsea's face. Mom walked over and enveloped her in her arms. "Baby, I'd die before I let anybody send you away from us. I love you so much it hurts. My mother was thinking of your best interests because she loves you too. Don't you ever think for one minute that you'd be sent away to boarding school," Mom assured her.

"Excellent," Pop proclaimed, winking at Jaris. "Now everything is back to normal. The artichokes are in the garbage. Grandma is riding her broom home. And all is well in the kingdom of the Spain clan."

"Lorenzo!" Mom snapped.

"Oh!" Pop said. "Did I say 'broom'? I meant to say 'convertible.'" Pop winked at Jaris again.

CHAPTER FIVE

The next day, Chelsea couldn't wait to get to Anderson to see Athena. She said she'd be back, and they could eat lunch again under the pepper trees. Chelsea had missed her so much. At lunch, Chelsea asked Athena, "Did that man who rescued me say anything when you gave him the reward?"

"No," Chelsea replied. "He was kinda scared. But he really looked amazed when he saw all that money. Athena, I'm so glad you're okay. I was scared you were never coming back,"

"Yeah," Athena agreed, opening her cheese and tomato sandwich, "I was really stupid. I thought the stuff in the bottle was just soda."

"Athena, what exactly did the boy look like—the one who gave you the liquor?" Chelsea pressed.

"Uh . . . he was like tall, and cute. He was really nice. He said he played football," Athena picked the tomato slice from her sandwich and threw the rest of it away. "I'm getting fat," she announced.

"No, you're not. You're too skinny," Chelsea protested.

"You know, Chel," Athena said, "I don't think that boy meant to hurt me. I don't think he knew there was liquor in that bottle."

"Yeah, but when you passed out, it was bad that he left you," Chelsea replied.

"You know," Athena explained, "it's all kinda fuzzy in my mind. I don't think he was even there anymore when I fainted. I think I took the drink from the sports bottle. Then we said goodbye, and he was gone before I got sick. I think that's what really happened. I don't think he had any idea what happened to me."

"Girl," Chelsea asserted, "I think you're making excuses for the guy 'cause he was cute and stuff. You don't want to believe anything bad about him."

"No way," Athena objected. "It's just I can't remember seeing him there just before I got sick."

"I think you're lying," Chelsea insisted. "I'm your best friend and you're lying to me."

Athena sighed. She looked sad and worried. Then finally she said, "Promise it stays between us if I tell you, Chel?"

"Yeah, promise," Chelsea assured her.

"I knew who the guy was," Athena confessed. "It's somebody you know, Chelsea. I didn't want to tell you who it was 'cause you used to like him a lot. And I thought it'd make you feel bad if he and I sorta liked each other now."

"Oh-my-gosh!" Chelsea gasped. "It's not Brandon Yates, is it? Please tell me it's not him!"

Brandon Yates was a freshman at Tubman whom Chelsea really liked. He had urged her to come to a party he was having, and Chelsea lied to her parents and went. It turned out to be a drug party, and Jaris dragged her home.

"Do you still like him, Chel?" Athena asked.

"No, I think he's a creep, Athena," Chelsea responded. "He used dope and stuff. And when I hung out with him I was in way over my head. We're just middle schoolers and it's dumb to hang with a guy from Tubman."

"He doesn't use dope anymore," Athena explained. "He's cleaned up his act, Chel. You'll keep your promise won't you? You won't tell anybody it was Brandon who gave me the liquor, will you? 'Cause he didn't know there was booze in that bottle. Somebody else must have poured the stuff in the bottle as a joke or something."

"I won't tell anybody," Chelsea pledged. "A promise is a promise. Have you talked to Brandon since that night?"

"Yeah, I texted him and told him what happened," Athena told her. "And he was all surprised and stuff. That's why I'm sure he wasn't there when I passed out. He was really sorry about there being liquor in the bottle, Chel."

"I think you're fooling yourself, girl, "Chelsea insisted. "I know he's cute and he can be real nice, but I bet he knew darn well what was in that bottle. And I bet when he saw you go down, he bailed. He's a liar, Athena. When he asked me to go to that party, he said it'd all be kids our age and stuff. When I got there, there were guys in their twenties. And B.J. Brady, that drug dealer, was passing stuff around. Brandon knew what he was getting me into. I just wish you weren't mixed up with him."

As she went home that day, Chelsea was sorry she had promised to keep Brandon's name a secret. She wasn't sure she should even keep that promise.

That night, when Pop came home, he had an announcement. "Old Jackson is selling the garage. He sprung it on me this afternoon. He's dumping the place."

"Selling the garage?" Mom repeated. "What does that mean for you, Lorenzo?"

Pop made an excellent salary working for Jackson. He had just gotten a big raise. He hated being a mechanic, but he was very good at it. Most of the customers came in because of Lorenzo Spain. He could fix just about any car and make it better than new. Pop answered, "Depends on who buys the place, Monie. If a dude with three mechanic sons comes along to buy the place, then I'm out of a job."

Pop sat down at the kitchen table. He looked at his wife and at Jaris, who had just come home from school. "Old Jackson asked me if I'd like to buy the place," he said.

"Lorenzo," Mom cried, "where would we get the money?"

"It's a gold mine down there, Monie," Pop said, deflecting the question. "With me in charge, it'd be even better. Jackson is a poor manager. He gets parts from the highest-priced guys and turns down chances to get parts that are cheaper and better quality. He keeps lousy books. We'd need to take out a loan on the house, Monie, but we'd get it paid off in no time,"

"A loan on the house?" Mom gasped. "We already have a mortgage. Lorenzo, that would be so dangerous. We could end up losing everything."

"That how much faith you got in your old man, girl?" Pop asked scornfully. "I'm telling you, I could pay back the money we'd need to borrow in a couple years. Heck, I could pay up the mortgage on the whole darn house in maybe three years. Monie, I want to do this. I know it's the right thing to do. If I let this chance pass, girl, I'm on the bottom rung of the ladder for keeps. This ain't my dream of going to college and being a scientist or something. That dream is dead and buried. But this is my chance to be more than a grease monkey doing the boss's bidding. This is my chance to be somebody, babe, to put my name out there on the garage—Spain's Auto Care, in big, bold letters."

Jaris's heart pounded with both fear and excitement. This could finally be his father's big chance. Maybe this was the only chance he'd ever get to be more than he was, to escape from the darkness, not to see himself as a loser anymore. "Pop, I think it'd be good," Jaris told him.

"See," Pop said. "My boy has faith in me. He's sixteen years old, and he has faith in his old man. I been married to you for almost eighteen years, Monie. And you're standing there shaking like I'm asking you to do a high wire act without a net. What's the matter with you, girl?"

"But Lorenzo, we could lose everything," Mom repeated. She wanted to believe in her husband. She loved him with all her heart. But he wanted to risk their home, their security, everything.

"Don't take this chance away from me, baby," Pop pleaded. "I'm pushing forty.

The train is comin' to the end of the tracks. Before I know it, the curtain comes down and I'm an old man who failed. Stand by me, girl. Life don't give a man many chances. I never thought I'd get a second one. But it's coming at me and I gotta grab it."

Chelsea had come home in the middle of the conversation. She grinned and said, "I want you to have the garage, Pop. It would be so exciting to see your name on it."

"See Monie, the little girl is on my side too," Pop declared. "Don't drag us all down." A hardness had come into the man's eyes. "And don't be running to the phone to whine to your mother that your husband wants to bring the family to ruin and pretty soon you'll be dumpster diving. Don't go whining to your mother like a child. This is not just my dream. It's for you and the kids too."

But late that night, Jaris heard his mother on the phone. Pop had gone to bed, and she was on her cell in the living room. "Oh Ma, I'm just sick. I don't know what to do. He has his heart set on it. I'm terrified that he'll fail. He's never run a business before. It's a whole other thing. He's a good mechanic, but can he run a business? . . . That's how I feel too, yes. Maybe overnight he'll give it more thought and come to his senses before it's too late. Maybe he'll get cold feet. Oh Mom, I'm so afraid we'll lose everything we've worked for, the house, the kids' college money. I make good money but I can't carry the whole thing, especially with a bigger mortgage. . . . Yes. . . . Okay Mom. . . .Thanks." She hung up.

Jaris came into the living room then.

"Grandma says not to do it, right?" Jaris asked.

"Jaris, are you spying on me now? Haven't I enough to deal with without you spying on me?" Mom complained.

"Mom," Jaris persisted, "don't fight Pop on this. He has to do it."

Anger leaked into Mom's eyes. "You've always been on his side, Jaris," she accused him. "You have this crazy belief that he's right in everything, but he isn't. I have to protect my family. I can't let this scatterbrained idea send us all into ruin."

"Grandma Jessie, she's all for throwing a monkey wrench into Pop's dream, right?" Jaris asked.

"My mother is an excellent business woman," Mom told Jaris in a cold voice. "When my father died, she took over everything and did much better than he ever did. She made a lot of money in real estate. She knows what she's talking about. She thinks Lorenzo'll run the garage into bankruptcy within a year, and I agree with her."

"Mom," Jaris insisted, "she's not our family. Our family is you and Pop and me and Chelsea. Your mom has no right to try to run our lives."

"Jaris, don't be lecturing me," Mom scolded. "You're just a boy. You're sixteen years old. You have this silly, romantic notion of your father charging into the business world and coming up a big winner.

But that's not him. *He's always been a loser.*" Mom's voice trailed off, and a stricken look came over her face. She seemed to desperately regret what she had just said, what she had said to her son, to Lorenzo's son. "I didn't mean that the way it came out, Jaris. I swear I didn't."

Jaris didn't say anything, but he thought, "Yeah, you did mean it, Mom. *You did mean it.* Because that's how you see Pop, and he knows it. That's part of the reason he sees himself as such a failure. His wife didn't have all that much faith in him, in his abilities, in his opinions, in his leadership of the family."

"Mom," Jaris responded, "give Pop a chance. Just give him a chance." Jaris turned then and went down the hall to bed. He didn't sleep very well. Mom had to cosign the application giving Pop the loan money he needed to buy the garage. If she stuck to her guns and didn't sign, then the dream was dead. Jaris wanted his father to have this chance. More than that, he knew what Mom's lack of support would do to the marriage. Jaris knew his parents loved each other, but a marriage needed more. It needed trust. Mom had to trust Pop. She had to be willing to go out on a limb with him. What if she killed his dream and he spent the rest of his life working as a grease monkey for another boss? How long would the love survive? Jaris was afraid to think about that.

At breakfast, Jaris asked Chelsea how Athena was doing.

"She's doing okay," Chelsea replied.

"She still can't remember more about the guy who gave her the liquor, huh?" Jaris asked.

"Uh, she said no," Chelsea lied, pouring milk on her oat cereal. She cut up some peaches and added them too. Then Chelsea spilled some milk on the table. She felt Jaris staring at her, as if he knew she wasn't telling the whole story. Chelsea was not a very good liar.

CHAPTER FIVE

As Chelsea was leaving for school, Jaris followed her. "Chili pepper, Athena knows the boy, doesn't she?" he asked.

"She says he, uh . . . looked familiar . . .," Chelsea replied, "but she thinks he made a mistake, that he didn't know the liquor was there in the bottle and stuff." Chelsea spotted Inessa who had come to walk to school with her. Chelsea smiled at Jaris and hurried out of the house to join Inessa.

"Hi Jaris," Inessa called out.

"Hi Inessa," Jaris answered, drawing closer. "You know Athena Edson, don't you?"

"Yeah," Inessa responded, "but I don't like her boyfriend. He's super icky." Chelsea gave Inessa a nudge but it was too late. The damage was already done.

"Who's her boyfriend?" Jaris asked.

Inessa knew she had said too much. "Uh, some guy who goes to Tubman," she said. Chelsea was glaring at her. "Come *on*, Inessa, we'll be late!" Chelsea said.

"What's his name, Inessa?" Jaris persisted.

"I just know his first name—Brandon something," Inessa replied. "He drives but he doesn't have a license."

Chelsea was dragging Inessa down the sidewalk now.

"Brandon Yates?" Jaris asked.

Inessa looked back, shrugged, and hurried along with Chelsea to Anderson Middle School.

As Jaris watched the girls go down the street, he could tell from Chelsea's body language that she was scolding Inessa for spilling too much. The hair on the back of Jaris's neck stood up. That little creep Brandon Yates was at it again, preying on middle schoolers. Brandon had chased Chelsea until Jaris ran him off. Now he was after Athena who didn't have a big brother to protect her. Jaris figured Brandon would be just the kind of creep who would get a girl drunk for the fun of it. Then he would bail when she passed out in the alley.

Jaris headed out for Tubman High. He planned to go over to the freshman lunch area and find Brandon Yates. He had confronted him once before, and Brandon seemed to scare easily. Maybe Jaris could scare him again.

During the lunch period that day, Jaris saw Brandon sitting alone on a bench and he called out, "Hey Yates, can I have a word with you, man?"

Brandon stood up, fear coming into his eyes. "Hey dude," he protested, "I got nothing to do with your sister. I ain't talked to her in a long time."

"I know," Jaris said. "Good thing too. But I'm talking about something else now. How come you gave a middle schooler liquor out of a sports bottle? Then when she passed out, you ran? Why'd you do that, man?" Jaris's voice was harsh as he came closer to the younger boy. Jaris was not one hundred percent sure Brandon was the culprit. He figured he would know for sure by Brandon's reaction to the accusation.

"I didn't!" Brandon insisted, turning ashen. "Anybody told you that is a liar. We were sharing the sports drink, me and a couple other guys. I didn't know what was in it. One of the other dudes musta spiked it. She was there, that chick, Athena. She goes, 'Lemme have a taste of that,' and she drinks it. She looked weird, and I didn't know what to do. So I cut out. I never saw her fall down, I swear."

"Oh yeah, that's a good story, Yates," Jaris snarled. "But lissen up, man. You stop hanging with girls from Marian Anderson Middle School. You hear me? You stop driving around there when you don't even have a license. You got no sense and you got no smarts, fool. You lissen to me, or I might just change your face in a way you won't like. Hear what I'm sayin'?"

"Yeah, I hear you," Brandon answered. He turned and joined a group of freshmen under the pepper trees. He kept looking back to see if Jaris was still standing there, staring at him. For a long time, Jaris was doing just that, just to put the fear in him.

CHAPTER SIX

Jaris turned and went back to the junior lunch area under the eucalyptus trees. Sereeta and Alonee Lennox were there. Oliver Randall had just walked up.

"I was going to come hunting for you, Jaris," Sereeta told him.

"Sorry I'm late," Jaris said to her. "I had to go over and give a freshman punk a hard time. He'd been chasing Chelsea, and now he's hanging around another kid. He gave this girl some liquor the other night, and she passed out behind a store. If a poor homeless guy hadn't found her, she might've been in big trouble. I told him I'd bust his face if he didn't stay away from the Anderson school kids."

"Good for you," Oliver said.

Trevor Jenkins joined the group as they were talking. "Parents shouldn't let their little thirteen-year-old girls hang out at the convenience store at night," he declared. "The girl I used to date, Vanessa Allen, that's what messed her up. She started hanging with guys when she was still a little girl, and she dropped outta school. Now her life is going downhill fast." There was a sad look on Trevor's face.

"Anybody know the Yates family?" Jaris asked. "I'd like to connect with them. This Brandon Yates needs to be reined in."

"There's a family by that name on my street," Sereeta offered. "Grandma sometimes mentions them. I'll find out tonight if Brandon lives there."

"Thanks, Sereeta," Jaris said, opening his lunch. He didn't have much appetite since Pop introduced the idea of buying the Jackson garage and Mom went ballistic.

Pop wasn't going to let that idea go, and Mom was stubborn too. Jaris honestly didn't know how it all would end.

That afternoon, as Jaris came jogging from school up to his home, he groaned. Grandma's red convertible was in the driveway. Usually she didn't come over during the week unless something important was going on. She knew Pop wouldn't be home for a while, but Mom was home from school. Jaris could guess what this visit was all about. Mom was complaining again about what she thought was Pop's harebrained idea to buy the garage. Grandma Jessie was here to back her up.

When Jaris came into the front room, he saw his mother and grandmother in animated conversation around the coffee table.

"Hi Jaris," Grandma Jessie said. "Did you have a nice day at school?"

"Wonderful," Jaris replied. "Couldn't be better." He knew he sounded sarcastic and he didn't care. He deeply resented his grandmother's efforts to manipulate his family. Why didn't she just stand back like other grandparents who let their sons and daughters handle their own problems? Mom was thirty-eight years old. And here was Grandma Jessie advising her as if she were eighteen.

"So," Grandma continued, as if Jaris weren't there, "you must stand firm, Monica. He will argue and try to bully you, but you cannot bend. Too much is at stake. This is not a clever man, your husband. When he tries to run a business, it will be a disaster. He will sink like a stone and take you and the children down with him."

"That's what I'm afraid of, Mom." Jaris's mother was speaking like a pliant little girl seeing the world from her mother's eyes.

"If I had any faith whatsoever in this man's business sense," Grandma Jessie said. "I would forward you the money myself. I'm not as well fixed as I used to be. My broker has made some disastrous mistakes, but still—"

"Oh Mom," Monica Spain objected, "I would never take money from you."

"Well," Grandma Jessie said, "I'm nearing seventy and one never knows what health problems, long range, lie ahead. I want to be prepared, and I certainly wouldn't invest in a scheme devised by Lorenzo. So, Monica, just tell him that the loan from the bank is out of the question. Just tell him to keep working at the garage. If he's laid off, he can find another job. Just tell him that he's a good mechanic. There's no disgrace in staying in that job for the rest of his working life. Tell him he has no right to risk his family's security."

"I will," Mom said compliantly.

Jaris stood in the hallway growing sicker by the minute. Mom sounded like a seven-year-old getting instructions from her mommy on how to handle a school problem.

"Lorenzo is not a boy anymore," Grandma Jessie went on. "He is old enough to realize his little ego trips must be behind him. The possibility that he would be a great success in life has passed him by years ago. The dreams are over. He must do his duty by his family."

Jaris couldn't hold himself back any longer. He threw caution to the winds. He came back into the living room and sat down in a chair opposite his mother and grandmother. He spoke quickly. "I've been listening to you, Grandma, and you're like writing my father off. He's too old for dreams. He's over the hill. He doesn't dare to do something new and exciting with his life. You have no faith in him. You don't like him. Well, we've always known that. But, Grandma, forgive me, but it's none of your freakin' business to write my father off."

Grandma Jessie looked shocked, but she kept her composure. "But it *is* my business," she insisted. "I love this family very much. Your father is toying with the financial security of my daughter, my only daughter, and my two grandchildren. And I am concerned."

"No, it's not your business," Jaris snapped. "Your daughter got married to Lorenzo Spain, and she and my pop should be making their own decisions. I hear you in here, Grandma, goin', 'Tell him this' and 'Tell him that.' And Mom is like 'Yes, Mom,' like a little kid. It makes me so mad I could puke. My mom has a master's degree in education. She's been teaching for like thirteen years, and twice she was voted the best elementary teacher in the district. When her principal has a big problem to solve, he comes here to ask for her input. He depends on her. Mom is probably gonna be a principal herself someday. She's a bright, educated, grown woman. What makes you think she doesn't know how to talk to her own husband?"

"Well," Grandma gasped, "I know your mother is an excellent teacher but—"

"But nothing!" Jaris cut in. "Grandma, I never asked you for a big favor. I mean, when I was five I asked you for a pony, and I understood why you didn't get me one.

But since then I've never asked. Now I'm asking you for a very big favor. Will you please butt out of my family's business?" Grandma Jessie and Mom sat in stunned silence. Jaris just went on.

"I love you and respect you, Grandma, but when my parents decide about buying or not buying the Jackson garage, let it be their decision, not yours. Give my family enough respect to leave us alone. Grandma, come and visit and bring cookies. Tell us stories about your childhood. Do what other grandmas do. Only please stop trying to control us."

Grandma Jessie put down her cup of green tea and stood up. She cast a scornful look at Jaris. She rolled her eyes at her daughter. Then she marched toward the door, letting herself out. In a few seconds the convertible was backing down the driveway with a speed uncharacteristic of Jessie Clymer.

Mom looked at Jaris. He was expecting a lecture on the need to respect one's elders, especially a grandmother. Jaris sat there, deciding to take it like a man, because he knew he was right. He did not regret a word he said.

Finally Mom spoke. "Jaris, I'm sure Mom was very hurt by what you said. . . . But, as I listened to you, I thought, 'Oh my goodness, he's a man. My little boy is a man.' "

Later, when it was time for Pop to come home from the garage, Mom's brow furrowed with worry. "I hope all this arguing hasn't put your father back into his old habits," she said, pretty much to herself. But Jaris and Chelsea could hear her.

Jaris and Chelsea remembered all too well when Pop would come home late from work. If he'd had a bad day, he would stop at a bar on the way home and have a few drinks with his friends. Then he would come home in a terrible mood, and everybody would scramble to get out of his way. That all ended when he went down to Pastor Bromley's church and took the pledge against drinking any more.

So far, Pop had kept his promise. He came home from work dirty, grumpy, and not smelling too good after a long day. But there was no alcohol on his breath. Jaris worried that he would break the promise today.

"He wants to buy that garage so much," Mom said, again within earshot of her children. "And I'm terrified of putting a bigger mortgage on the house. It's like we're between a rock and a hard place. We went back and forth so long last night that maybe he . . ."

Every time a car turned down the street, all three of them looked out the window and waited for the familiar sound of Pop's truck grinding down the driveway. You couldn't mistake his arrival from anyone else's.

"Several people we knew had their homes foreclosed," Mom said, finally speaking directly to Jaris and Chelsea. "It's such a terrible feeling to be deep in debt."

Then they all froze when the sound of Pop's pickup hit the driveway. The truck door slammed.

"Hey everybody!" Pop greeted them. He was walking tall. "Old Jackson spent some time today showing me the books. He don't put anything on the computer. The man is living in the Stone Age. I'm computerizing all the stuff. He runs the place like it's a covered wagon way station. A friend of mine, Cy Bentley, he's a CPA. I've got an appointment with the dude. He's smart. He's coming over to the garage and look at all the books, get things up to speed." Pop looked at Mom then, and he put up his hand as if to deflect any objections.

"Not that we've decided if we're going to buy the place yet. We're still in the talking stage. But if it's a go, I want to be ready." He smiled and said, "Gotta shower now and make something good for dinner. No pulling dinner from the freezer tonight." He headed for the bathroom whistling.

When Jaris was in his room working on his computer, Chelsea looked in. "You really messed me up today," she told him.

"Did I? How so?" Jaris asked, although he knew.

"Athena won't even talk to me," Chelsea said.

"That can't be all bad," Jaris kidded her.

"You don't understand!" Chelsea complained. "She thinks I ratted her out and told you about Brandon."

"Didn't you tell her Inessa spilled the beans by mistake, chili pepper?" Jaris asked.

"She didn't even give me the chance. She turned her back on me," Chelsea said.

Jaris looked at his sister and posed the question he wanted to ask. "Is Athena really hanging out big time with Brandon Yates?"

Chelsea shrugged. "A little bit."

"Well," Jaris confessed, "I'm sorry to tell you, chili pepper. I told the creep to lay off the little girls from Anderson or I'll give him a new face, one he won't like as much as the one he's used to."

"Jaris, who do you think you are?" Chelsea cried. "The boss of everybody?"

"A man's gotta do what a man's gotta do," Jaris insisted. Chelsea turned and stomped out of the room and into her bedroom, slamming the door after her.

Late in the night, again Jaris heard his parents talking about Jackson's garage. He heard snatches of conversation because his bedroom was next to theirs.

"But, Lorenzo, you have no business experience," Mom was saying.

"When Jackson goes on vacation, I pay all the bills," Pop told her.

"But to have all that responsibility on your back . . . "

"All my life I've wanted something better than what I got," Pop said. "Every day I go to work, get dirty, get yelled at, I look up at that sign over the big doors: Jackson's Auto Repair. It could say Spain's Auto Care. I could be the boss."

"Lorenzo, you've been a success in so many other ways already."

"No, I been a loser, babe," Pop insisted. "Ever since I didn't get that chance to go to college and be somebody, I been a loser. But this would make a difference. I could be proud of something, Monie. I could own a business. I could join the Chamber of Commerce and drink coffee and mingle with the big muckety-mucks . . . "

After a while, there was silence. Jaris lay there, staring at the ceiling. He knew there was a chance Mom and Pop'd take out a mortgage to buy the business, Pop would fail, and he'd lose the garage. There was always a chance of something like that happening. But still he wanted Pop to have the chance. If he didn't get it, then pretty soon it would dawn on him that his last chance went by and nothing would ever be any different for him, except that he was getting older. He'd be an aging loser with more gray hair, a slump to his shoulders, and a job working for other, more successful men.

Jaris wanted his father to buy the garage as much as his father wanted to. Lorenzo Spain had been living in a kind of darkness, a belief that life was basically unfair and that the cards were stacked against some people. If you were a loser, you stayed a loser, and life beat you down until there was nothing left but bitterness. Sometimes Jaris bought into this idea, and he wondered if the darkness would envelop him too. Jaris was trying to outrun the darkness. If his Pop could, then maybe he could too.

At school the next day, Sereeta told Jaris, "Yeah, Brandon belongs to the Yates family on our street. They have older kids who live in Los Angeles. A couple of them have been busted for drugs. Grandma thinks the place is a drug house sometimes. The guys come from LA in really big cars. Real flashy. Everybody keeps waiting for a big police raid or something."

"Oh brother!" Jaris groaned. "It sure wouldn't do much good to talk to the parents about straightening Brandon out."

"Doesn't sound like a plan," Sereeta agreed.

"Well, thanks for the information," Jaris said. "I've just gotta keep leaning on that dude to quit goin' over to the middle school."

"Speaking of parents," Sereeta mentioned, "my mom has texted me like every day this week. She feels really bad that she didn't come to the birthday party we girls planned for her. She told me she was wasted, but she swears she's trying to quit that stuff. She wants to make amends, Jaris. Am I . . . uh . . . an idiot to have some hope here?"

"No Sereeta, you have to follow your heart," Jaris told her softly.

"She's wanting to spend Sunday with me," Sereeta continued, "you know, time for us. There's a little voice inside my head that says, 'Don't go there.' I'm afraid I'll just get hurt all over again. Still, *she's my mom*. I can't completely get over that. There's this thing in me that wants a mom, even a little bit of a mom. I mean, anything she can give me. I feel sometimes like a stray dog running after its former owner, begging for a little pat on the head. It's like depression and I hate that feeling. What do you really think, Jaris?"

Sereeta's beautiful eyes were filled with hope as Jaris had seen so many times before. And he had seen the hope dashed, again and again. Sereeta looked at him now, silently pleading for him to urge her to try one more time.

Jaris took Sereeta in his arms, holding her tightly. He brushed a kiss over the top of her curly hair. "Babe," he assured her, "taking a risk is okay. It's better to take a risk even if you lose. It's better than not to try at all and maybe lose something much more precious."

"You think I should tell her yes," Sereeta asked in a shaky voice, "that we can go somewhere this Sunday? She didn't say where we'd go. But she said she wanted to make it up to me for all the times she'd disappointed me. I sorta feel like that kid in the *Peanuts* cartoon. You know he keeps trying to kick the ball, and he hopes Lucy won't whisk it away and make him stumble and fall again."

"Go for it, babe," Jaris told her.

Sereeta smiled at him. "*I love you so much*," she gushed.

CHAPTER SEVEN

The next day, all during Mr. Pippin's English class, Jaris thought about Sereeta. Her parents divorced when she was in middle school, and the divorce devastated her. Both her parents remarried. She had little to do with her father and his new wife. Her mother and stepfather had had a new baby, and Sereeta felt excluded from their lives. Sereeta's stepfather tried to send her away to a boarding school where she would have lost all her friends at Tubman High. But Sereeta's grandmother took her in, and now Sereeta was almost happy. But she still longed for the closeness with her mother that she had lost. Every time Sereeta reached out to her mother, she was rebuffed. Now her mother was reaching out, and Jaris hoped it wouldn't be another bitter disappointment.

When Jaris got home from school, Chelsea was sitting on the curb in front of the house with Heston Crawford. Chelsea was wearing short-shorts and a skimpy halter top. "Hey," Jaris hailed as he passed the pair.

"Hey yourself," Chelsea responded.

"Pop's coming home early, chili pepper. Jackson is giving him half the day off so he's got more time to figure out a deal to buy the garage," Jaris told her.

"So?" Chelsea said in a snippy voice.

"Just letting you know," Jaris said, continuing on into the house. In a few minutes Pop's pickup turned the corner. He slowed down and pulled into the driveway. Jaris heard his voice, "Hey, little girl, did you forget to put on your clothes?"

Jaris winced.

"Pop," Chelsea cried, "it's almost summer! I didn't wear these clothes to school. They're too casual."

Pop got out of the cab of the truck. "So you put on the itty bitty clothes so's you can play with the little punk here?" he demanded. Pop turned his angry glare to Heston, "Who're you anyway?"

"Heston Crawford," the boy said in a startled voice.

"So, you go to Anderson Middle School too?" Pop went on. "You're pretty tall. You sure you're not one of those ninth-grade bums from Tubman preying on the little girls at Anderson?" Pop was standing there, towering over the two teenagers on the curb. Pop was covered with grease and grime and perspiration, making his rugged features look even more menacing.

"No sir, I'm an eighth grader from Anderson," Heston replied.

"Little girl," Pop commanded, "go inside the house and put some clothes on. The whole neighborhood is out looking at you. See the guy across the street? He was watering his lawn, now his eyes are popping out of his head. See him ogling you over here?"

"Pop, I'm not a little girl," Chelsea cried. "And nobody is looking at me!" Her voice rose to almost a scream, "It's almost summer—"

"Yeah, you said that already," Pop yelled back. "Lord help us when summer really comes. You gonna skip dressing altogether and romp around in your birthday suit, little girl? Look at this little punk here sitting with you. He can't keep his eyes off you. He can't even get enough of you. He's droolin'. See how he's droolin' there?"

Heston looked terrified. He'd never met anyone quite like Chelsea's father. "I-I was just looking at that cat that just went up the tree, sir," he stammered. "I really like cats."

"Don't be changing the subject," Pop growled. "This little girl here has suddenly gone wild. She don't like putting real clothes on. She wants the whole neighborhood to have a show looking at her. Some of the window shades flippin' now. Folks wanting a look."

"Hey," Heston commented, looking at the watch on his skinny wrist. "It's getting late. Ma said to be home early. Got chores. Taking out the trash and stuff . . . takes some time. Lotta trash. Uh . . . Chel, see you in science. Uh, nice meeting up with you, Mr. Spain, real nice." Heston jumped up and took off, sprinting away. He never looked back.

Chelsea glared at her father. "Pop, why are you deliberately humiliating me in front of my friends from school?" she demanded to know.

"Hey little girl—" Pop began.

"I'm not a little girl anymore," Chelsea yelled. "Stop calling me that."

"Hey, don't remind me," Pop said. "Just a while ago you were a skinny little thing. Looked like a boy. Now you're spreading out in all directions, getting those curves. Only you don't want to cover them up. And that Heston character, boy, his eyes were popping right out of his head. I know that kind, Chelsea. I was once one of them."

Mom came out then. "What's all the fuss about?" she asked.

"Oh, this little girl here," Pop explained, "she's sitting on the curb with some punk, says he's an eighth grader. I'm not so sure. He's eatin' her up with his big eyes 'cause look how she's dressed. Itty bitty pants, skimpy little straps there—don't' cover much. 'Course that's the whole idea."

Chelsea ran into the house and to her bedroom, slamming the door so hard the house seemed to shake. Jaris said from the hallway, "Chili pepper, didn't I warn you he was coming? I warned you and you gave me a snippy 'so.' "

Chelsea opened the door to complain. "Jaris, how long is he gonna be this way? He's driving me crazy. It just dawned on my pop that I'm growing up and he's freaking!"

"He's worried, chili pepper," Jaris told her. "He loves you very much. He's worried that some creepy boy is going to hurt you one way or the other."

"Heston is a nice guy, Jaris," Chelsea protested. "He's really shy. And Pop goes off on like he's some maniac who's after me."

"It's hard for parents, chili pepper," Jaris explained. "Especially when you got a girl. It's a jungle out there. Some nice guys, a lot not so nice. Look at what happened to Athena. That could have been the end of the road for her. And all because of some stupid jerk like Brandon Yates."

"He didn't mean for that to happen, Jaris," Chelsea said.

"That's a crock," Jaris corrected her. "He gave liquor to a kid. I don't believe that story that somebody else put the booze in his bottle. I don't believe it for a minute. He thought it'd be fun to make her drunk, and when she passed out, the little creep bailed. If Athena buys that, she's one dumb little chick."

Chelsea put her hands on her hips and glared at her brother. "Is that what you think I am too, a dumb little chick?" she demanded.

"Sometimes, yeah," he agreed. "You make better grades than me, chili pepper. And you'll probably ace high school and get honors in college. But when it comes to boys, you girls are sitting ducks, and creepy guys know it."

"Oh!" Chelsea snapped. "You're getting more like him every day, like Pop. What good does it do to reason with either of you?" She went back in her room, slamming the door even harder than before.

Pop was in the kitchen making dinner. He was merrily banging the pots and pans. Jaris was trying to do his homework when another argument broke out between his parents.

"You've got to ease up on Chelsea, Lorenzo," Mom told Pop. "You're making her crazy."

"Yeah," Pop agreed, "that makes two of us. She's making me crazy too. This here's gonna be a Mexican polenta pie. We never had one of them."

"Lorenzo," Mom went on, "you are making her so upset that she won't bring her friends home anymore."

"Oh no!" Pop cried in mock horror. "You mean those beady-eyed little punks won't be coming around drooling over her in her mini clothes anymore? So, let's see, we mix up the cornmeal, water, and salt, and we let it boil."

"Lorenzo, you are getting impossible," Mom said. "You are getting like Mickey Jenkins. Next thing you know you'll be knotting wet towels and beating Chelsea, the way she beat her boys."

"Hey!" Pop exclaimed. "Now that's not a bad idea. One thing for sure, Mickey didn't raise any bums. She raised four great boys in a tough neighborhood without a man to help her. Two of them in the army serving the country, one in college, and Trevor, a great kid too. So whatever she's doing, she's doing fine."

He opened up a can of beans. "Don't these look good? Hey Monie, once I get the garage, maybe I'll open up an eatery too. I could fix cars and dish out grub too. I'd be a double threat man, babe."

"It's all a big joke to you, isn't it?" Mom commented bitterly.

"No, I'm dead serious, Monie," Lorenzo Spain replied. "I'm gonna see the banker next week and talk turkey. We got to sign the loan then, you and me. Both our names on the property and we both gotta sign on the dotted line. Then I'm a businessman, no longer just a grease monkey."

"What if I just can't?" Mom asked in a suddenly emotional voice.

"You mean you wouldn't sign?" Pop asked. There was a terrible gravity to his voice.

"What if I just can't take the chance of losing it all?" Mom asked him in return.

"That'd be telling me you don't trust me, Monie," Pop told her. "That'd be saying your man has just one last chance to be somebody, to be a man. That'd be saying he needs his wife's support, but you won't give it to me. That'd be turning your back on me, babe. I'm not sure I could come back from that."

Mom sounded like she was about to cry. "What are you saying, Lorenzo?" she cried.

"You heard me," he said.

"So you're threatening me," Mom argued. "Either I sign or we're over. Is that it?"

Jaris froze. He felt like putting his hands over his ears because he didn't want to hear the answer. But he listened.

"I don't know, babe. I really don't know," Pop responded. "If you're not on my side . . . if the person I love more than anybody else on earth isn't behind me, I don't know what would happen. You're my woman, Monie. I love the kids more than my own life. But if you're not with me, if you won't help me carry the dream, then I'm not sure I got the stuff to go on."

There was a deep, almost dreadful silence. Then Jaris heard his father stirring the cornmeal and whipping in an egg. Then he spread the cornmeal in a pie plate, spread the beans over the cornmeal, and sprinkled cheese and corn chips over everything.

The Mexican polenta pie was delicious, but the atmosphere around the table was tense. Chelsea was sulking about being humiliated in front of Heston. Jaris was sick about the conversation between his parents that he had overheard. Mom and Pop seemed lost in their own separate worlds, almost like enemies across a battlefield, waiting for the other side to fire the first shot.

That night Jaris heard his parents in the hallway on their way to bed. "The dinner was delicious, Lorenzo," Mom remarked. "You're a great cook."

"Thanks, babe," Pop responded.

"I'm tired," Mom said. "It was a hard day at school."

"Yeah, at the garage too," Pop said. Then he told her, "No matter what happens, I'll always love you. You know that, don't you, babe?"

Jaris could tell his mother was crying, though her sounds were muffled. Her face was pressed against Pop's chest.

On Monday, Jaris was anxious to see Sereeta to find out how her Sunday with her mother had gone. There had been no phone call, no texting from Sereeta. Jaris was afraid that was a bad sign—an indication that her mom had let her down again.

But when Jaris arrived on the Tubman campus, Sereeta came running toward him, a big smile on her face. "Oh Jaris, we didn't get back till three this morning," she said excitedly. "It was just so amazing!"

"Wow," Jaris replied, glad to see the radiant look of happiness on her face.

"We flew to San Francisco!" Sereeta cried. "Just Mom and me. It was crazy. It was wonderful. We stayed in this beautiful old hotel, and we went to Chinatown and had the most awesome dinner. We walked all around, and we bought souvenirs and laughed and talked. I felt like I was eleven years old again, having fun with my mom. It was so fabulous. It was like the old days when Mom and me did fun things together. Like we used to get up in the middle of the night and go down to the beach when the grunions were running—those tiny silver fish. Mom was so happy then and I was happy too . . . it was before all the bad stuff happened."

Jaris gave Sereeta a big hug. "I'm so glad you had a good time, babe."

"Jaris, she was my mother again," Sereeta confided. "We got lost once and we laughed until our sides ached. Then we almost missed our plane, and they made us take off our shoes, you know, for security at the airport. Mom broke a heel and she giggled about that too. Oh Jaris, I'll never *ever* forget it. You know, my grandma said that, when Grandpa died, she thought if she could have had one more great day with him, then she'd be able to cope better with him being gone. One amazing day to remember, and that's how it was with me and mom. Well, no matter what happens now, I'll have this day to remember. I didn't have any good memories of these last years. But now this is like a gift, a treasure I'll never forget."

"Sereeta, that's great. You deserved it," Jaris said.

Sereeta was still savoring her day with her mom. "When Mom doesn't pay any attention to me again. And when I miss her, I'll feel her arms around me and that wonderful perfume she wears will be all around me. I'll feel like Mom's kid again. And, you know what, Jaris? When she asked me to come with her this weekend, I almost turned her down. I just didn't want to be hurt again. But you gave me the courage to try again, Jaris. You told me to follow my heart. I woulda told Mom no, and I woulda missed all this. And now I've got still another reason to love you, Jaris, because you make me strong when I'm weak."

When they all had lunch under the eucalyptus trees that day, Sereeta regaled them with her adventures in San Francisco. Alonee and Oliver, Kevin and Carissa, Derrick and Destini, and Sami and Matson listened and laughed with her and rejoiced with her. It dawned on Jaris that he had never seen Sereeta quite so lovely as she was right now. Her face glowed with joy.

Sereeta's mother had bought her a small replica of a San Francisco cable car. That Sunday was just a brief moment in the months and years of sadness. But it would stay in Sereeta's memory as something to warm her heart when the days and nights turned cold. And as long as Sereeta lived, she would keep the little cable car on her bedroom dresser.

CHAPTER EIGHT

"Look!" Athena shouted when school let out at Marian Anderson Middle School. "Did you ever see a car like that? It's like a silver chariot!"

It was a silver Mercedes. Chelsea and Inessa stretched their necks for a look at the car as it cruised down the street.

"Brandon Yates is sitting next to the driver," Inessa noted.

"Who's driving?" Keisha asked. Keisha was a cheerleader at Anderson and a friend of Chelsea's.

"That's Cory Yates, Brandon's brother," Athena answered. "He said he'd be down this week from LA. He's really rich."

"How did he get so rich?" Inessa asked, wrinkling her nose. "He's real young. I bet he's a crook."

"Oh Inessa," Athena laughed, "you're such a wet blanket, girl."

The Mercedes turned around and came back down the street adjoining the school. Brandon grinned out at Athena, Chelsea, Keisha, and Inessa. "You chicks want a ride around the block in a cool car?" he yelled.

"Oh wow," Athena said, quivering with excitement. "I never in my whole life rode in a car like that. I bet it cost thousands and thousands of dollars! I'd feel like a princess!"

"You'd be a fool, Athena," Inessa advised. "Gettin' in that car is gonna be nothin' but bad."

"Oh, it'd be so exciting," Keisha exclaimed, grabbing Chelsea's hand.

"If my pop ever found out," Chelsea groaned, "he'd lock me in the closet until I turned eighteen."

"He won't know. It's just a spin around the block," Athena said.

Keisha tugged on Chelsea's hand. "Come on, girl! I so wanna go, but I won't go unless you come too." Keisha was jumping up and down with excitement as the big silver car pulled to the curb in front of them. "Oh please, *please*, Chelsea!"

"Keisha, my pop!" Chelsea gasped.

"You guys," Inessa warned, "you're crazy if you get in that car with those whacko boys."

"Just a little ride, Chelsea," Keisha begged. "I never in my whole life rode in anything better than a rusty old Toyota, and maybe I never will!"

Athena got into the Mercedes first, squealing with excitement, followed by Keisha and Chelsea. Keisha still held tightly to Chelsea's hand. The door slammed shut.

Cory Yates looked back at the girls and smiled. He was even handsomer than his little brother, Brandon. He wore cool shades and designer jeans. He immediately turned on the music, a pounding rap. The whole car seemed to shudder with the angry beat. Cory was snapping his fingers and rolling his head from side to side with the music.

"What're you sayin' 'freeze?' " a raucous male voice demanded in the song, "takin' me down with the greatest of ease. Whatcha doin' in my hood? What made you think you could?"

Cory looked back, grinning, and sped up.

> This is my hood, and you better
> believe it,
> You're not the man I am,
> If you cross me, you gonna grieve it.

Keisha looked out the window at the kids from Anderson, some of them her friends, staring at her going by in a silver Mercedes. "Chel," Keisha cried, "look! They'd give anything to be where we are. Look at how they're looking at us! They're envying us, girl. It's like having a snow cone on a hot day when nobody else has one!"

Chelsea spotted just one face in the crowd of surprised classmates. Inessa was looking upset. Inessa was a very good girl. She never gave her parents a moment's worry. Chelsea often thought Pop should have had Inessa as a daughter instead of her.

Athena waved at the gawking kids. "Eat your hearts out," she screamed happily.

"Athena, don't!" Chelsea pleaded. "They'll get even with us."

"Look," Keisha laughed. "Lark Lennox is getting picked up by her mom. Look how jealous she looks!"

Chelsea saw Maya Archer getting picked up too. Maya saw Chelsea in the Mercedes, and she had a look of disbelief on her face. Chelsea began to get a little nervous. What if somebody texted Pop or called Mom? Chelsea hoped the Mercedes would turn around quickly and return to school, dropping her and the others off.

Brandon had said just a "ride around the block."

But the Mercedes was free of the school traffic now. Instead of turning around, it was roaring up the freeway ramp. Cory Yates turned up the volume of the rap music even louder. The Mercedes itself seemed to be rocking to the beat.

Lissen up suckas, you got nothin'
to lose,
Smoke what you like, and jack the
booze.
World comin' down in a mighty blast,
Fool, didja think this all would last?

"Where are we going?" Chelsea screamed at the driver, trying to be heard above the din.

"Cory wants to show you what this baby can do on the open road," Brandon shouted. "We're gonna be flyin', babe." Once on the freeway, the Mercedes scooted across lanes amid a wild chorus of honking horns.

"Get outta my way, suckas," Cory shouted. To her horror, Chelsea recognized in Cory some of the signs she saw in the guests at that party that Jaris had dragged her from months ago. Cory was high on something.

"We're doin' over a hundred miles an hour, gang," Cory shouted. "Hey, we almost taking off into outer space like a rocket ship."

Keisha looked scared for the first time since the ride started. She was thinking that maybe Inessa was right and that this all was a big mistake. Chelsea was thinking the same thing.

"Wheee!" Athena was screaming as the Mercedes chewed up the freeway, passing every car in sight. The rap music powered on again,

Lissen man, you're on your way,
 nobody stopping you, you can play.
Winner's circle just ahead,
Never quit 'till you're good and dead!

"Slow down!" Chelsea yelled, grabbing Brandon's shoulder. "Make your brother slow down! We'll all be killed!"

Brandon looked back. He was on something too. His eyes looked bad. "You wanna live forever, chick?" he asked, laughing.

Keisha grabbed Chelsea's hand for comfort. Keisha's eyes were so big with fright that they seemed to fill her entire face. Chelsea was shaking with terror too. She thought they would crash at any moment in a mangled inferno. Chelsea remembered all the wrecked cars she had seen in recycling yards—the jagged steel twisted into the passenger's area. She had always shivered at the thought of how the people died in those cars or how they were permanently scarred and disabled. Chelsea remembered a TV news spot about a little nine-year-old girl whose neck was broken in a car accident; she would spend the rest of her life unable to move her arms and legs.

Chelsea kept asking herself, "Why did I risk this? Why did I get in this car? Why did

I risk my health and my life for a stupid ride in a silver Mercedes? I could be in intensive care tonight, paralyzed for life, lying in a coma. I could be missing an arm or a leg. Or I could be blind or dead in the morgue . . . "

"Slow down," Chelsea screamed with all her might. "You'll get us all killed!"

Even Athena looked a little worried now. Until now she was enjoying the thrill of the ride, but now she added her own pleas. "Brandon, tell your brother to slow down."

Cory Yates did slow down momentarily as he left the freeway and continued on a two-lane country road. He looked back at the three girls clinging together in terror. And he threw back his head and laughed. "Hey, you chicks, bet you never been on a ride like this, not even in the amusement park! Don't this beat the roller coasters? This is the real world!"

The Mercedes was flying down the country road at over ninety miles an hour. Cars coming in the opposite direction looked like blurs of color when he passed them. The trees on the sides of the road blended into walls of green.

Up ahead, a car was doing about fifty. Cory slowed a little and hit the horn, screaming, "Outta my way, sucka. Get off the road, fool. If you're gonna creep along like this, you don't belong drivin'!"

The car ahead continued at its same speed, and Cory began frantically trying to pass in the oncoming lane. Every time he cut out to pass, oncoming traffic forced him back behind the slower car. He was getting hysterical. He honked nonstop at the frightened driver ahead. The driver was an elderly man who just kept going fifty miles an hour. Then Cory saw an opening. He swerved into the oncoming lane, passing the slower car and screaming at the elderly driver as he did.

"There's a car coming!" Chelsea screamed. She covered her face with her hands. They were going to crash head-on with the oncoming car. That was it.

A grinding head-on collision. For just one horrible second Chelsea imagined herself lying in her silk-lined casket at Holiness Awakening Church with Mom and Pop and Jaris standing there crying. Her lips moved soundlessly now, "I'm so sorry . . . so sorry . . ."

The oncoming car swerved onto the shoulder of the road to avoid the hurtling Mercedes. The Mercedes flew past and returned to its own lane.

"See what that slow movin' sucka almost caused?" Cory yelled bitterly.

Chelsea had her cell phone in her purse. She thought of calling the police, but then there would be a police chase, like when the cops were chasing B.J. Brady—and he crashed in flames. "Please let us out," Chelsea cried. "Please let Keisha, Athena, and me out."

"Here?" Cory laughed. They were in the middle of a woodland area. There were no houses nearby.

"Just let us out!" Chelsea pleaded.

Ahead, there was a small store bearing a large sign, "Beer, Wine, Spirits." Cory slowed down and eased the Mercedes into the parking lot in front of the store. "You girls sit tight," he ordered them. "Me and Brandon gonna get some refreshments. You chicks want some sodas?"

"Nothing," Chelsea told him.

"Okay," Cory said. "Soon's we come out, we'll take you back to the school. Ain't even gonna charge you for this fun ride, chicks."

Chelsea's heart was madly pounding. She thought she might have a heart attack before she was killed in a car accident.

When the boys disappeared into the store, Chelsea looked at Keisha. They both looked at Athena. They had come close to something terrible happening. But they had survived. Chelsea pushed the door open. Keisha tumbled out after her, then Athena. They hit the ground running. They didn't know what Cory and Brandon would do when they found them gone. Both boys were high. They might try to find them and force them back into the Mercedes. So the girls kept running until they reached a thick stand of trees.

"I can see them coming out of the store," Chelsea reported. "They're looking around for us."

Cory and Brandon were drinking from bottles they just bought. Now they would be drunk as well as drugged. The boys looked around a bit more. Then they got into the Mercedes and roared off. Chelsea pulled out her cell phone and called the highway patrol. She told them there was a silver Mercedes out on the country road heading east and gave a description of the car and the guys in it.

"I can't believe we got in that car with those freakin' stoned guys," Keisha exclaimed.

"I didn't think Brandon's brother would drive like that," Athena added. "It was crazy!"

Chelsea looked at her watch. "I shoulda been home an hour ago. My bike is still at school. My folks must be going crazy by now."

"Mine too," Keisha moaned. "Mom's gonna kill me."

Chelsea got on her cell phone. The last thing in the world she wanted to do was call her parents and tell them what happened. But she had no choice. She was almost as afraid of Pop's reaction as she was of getting pulverized in the Mercedes.

"Mom?" Chelsea said when she heard her mother's voice. Mom sounded frantic.

"Chelsea! Oh thank God! Are you okay, baby?" Mom cried. She sounded like she had been crying.

"I'm okay, Mom," Chelsea assured her. "I'm fine. Athena and Keisha are with me, and they're okay too. We're out here in the country by a little store."

Chelsea heard her father's voice in the background. "Gimme the phone, Monie." When he came on, he sounded gruff. "Chelsea?"

"I'm here, Pop," Chelsea replied. She had no feeling in her legs. She felt like she would collapse at any moment into a pile of quivering gelatin.

"Are you guys in a safe place?" Pop asked.

"Yeah, we're by this store and the . . . the guys who were driving us in the car . . . they're, uh, gone," Chelsea told him.

"Inessa called us the minute you guys got in the Mercedes," Pop said. "We called Keisha's parents but we couldn't get a hold of Athena's idiot parents. Look, tell me exactly where you are."

Chelsea and the other two girls walked up to the store and told Pop the address that was printed on the outside of the building. "It's 391 Smoky Lane Highway," Chelsea told him.

"My Lord," Pop gasped. "You're thirty miles from school. Okay, listen to me. Go in the store and stay there. Don't leave the place. Tell the people there what happened and wait where it's safe. We're on our way."

"An old man and his wife run the store," Chelsea said to her dad. "I see them in there. It looks like a man and his wife."

"Okay," Pop replied. "We called the cops right away when Inessa called us. The cops have been looking for you. So now I'm gonna tell them you're okay. So, like I said, we're on our way."

The three girls went into the store and bought candy bars and sodas.

"My parents are gonna come down on me like a ton of bricks," Keisha groaned. "Your pop called them, Chelsea, and they know what we did. I bet my parents take away my TV, my computer, and who knows what else."

Athena shrugged. "It won't be that bad for me. My mom is so busy teaching high school that she hasn't got time to bug me. And Dad's even worse. He works day and night. You know, when that thing happened in the alley, they didn't punish me or anything. They were real nice about it. They just hugged me." Athena smiled a little.

Then she said, "Now that it's all over, you guys, it *was* kinda exciting, wasn't it? I mean, I've never been in a car going that fast—and a Mercedes! It was almost kinda unreal. I think Cory was doing one ten or something."

Chelsea glared at Athena. Chelsea almost screamed at her. "It wasn't exciting. It was horrible. I was sick the whole time. What if we'd smashed up? We could be spending the rest of our lives lying in a bed with nurses feeding us and changing our diapers. I'm only fourteen years old! I got a lot of stuff I wanna do. I got a life ahead of me. I don't wanna throw it all away for a stupid ride in some dopehead's Mercedes. I hate myself for going along with you guys. Inessa was right. I shoulda stuck with her."

"Oh," Athena laughed, "you can't be an old fraidy cat or life is dull."

Keisha frowned and said, "Chelsea is right. What we did was stupid. It was worse than stupid."

"I totally hate Brandon Yates," Chelsea added. "If I ever see him again, I'm gonna spit in his dirty face. And, Athena, you're a big fool if you have anything to do with him anymore. He knew what he and his brother would do, and he lured us into the car."

"Aw, Brandon's not a bad guy," Athena objected.

"He's scum. He's lowdown scum," Chelsea asserted. "And stop lying to yourself, girl. He gave you that liquor. When you passed out in the alley, he ran. He left you laying there where the rats might have chewed on your face. That's the kind of person he is."

Athena said nothing. She looked off into the distance, sadly. "Brandon said he loved me," she confided. "Nobody else says that to me . . . not even my parents."

The girls settled down to wait for Chelsea's dad to pick them up.

CHAPTER NINE

"There's my pop," Chelsea said after a long wait, a tremor in her voice. She turned numb.

Pop was driving Jaris's Honda Civic. There wouldn't be room enough for the three girls in Pop's pickup, and Jaris's mom wasn't home from work when Pop got the call. Jaris was sitting beside Pop.

Chelsea was deeply ashamed even to face her father. The Civic pulled into the parking lot of the store, and Chelsea's dad and brother got out. Pop was on his cell phone to Mom. "Yeah, babe, I see them right now. They're coming out of the store, the three of them. They look fine. . . . Yeah. Take it easy. No need to cry now, babe.

Everything's okay. Listen, you call Keisha's parents, okay? Tell 'em I'm bringing her. Tell 'em she's on her way home. And try to get Athena's idiot parents. Tell the fools if they don't answer, we're dropping the kid off at child protective."

Pop and Jaris came walking toward the three girls. Pop's stare settled on Athena first. "What makes me think this little caper was your idea?" He didn't wait for an answer. "Everybody in the car," Pop commanded them. "We got an hour's drive ahead of us. We ain't goin' to be drivin' no hundred miles an hour like the creep was."

The three girls got into the backseat and put on their seat belts. They were crowded. As Pop pulled out, he reported., "It was all over the radio, a silver Mercedes goin' on the freeway over a hundred miles an hour, scattering traffic like chickens. The cops were on it, but the dopehead left the freeway before the cops spotted him. Inessa called us right after you three fools got in the Mercedes and took off from school. That's a good girl there. She described the car and said Brandon Yates's zonked-out brother was driving. Can you imagine what me and your mom were going through, little girl? And Keisha, your folks too?"

"I'm sorry Pop," Chelsea apologized. "I really am."

Pop ignored her. "Your mom, Chelsea, she's been tearing her hair out. You gave her a lot of grief."

Jaris glanced into the backseat and met Chelsea's gaze. He didn't say anything, but Chelsea knew what was going through his mind. Once he rescued Chelsea from a drug party Brandon Yates had lured her into. In stern terms he had warned her to stay away from Yates. And now she did this. She got into a car driven by Yates's brother, and she could have been killed. Jaris looked disappointed and angry, but he said nothing.

After a long, silent drive, Pop pulled up in the driveway where Keisha's parents lived. They were both outside, rushing to claim their daughter. As Keisha got out of the car, her mother embraced her sobbing, saying over and over, "Oh baby, my baby!"

Keisha's father said grimly, "Girl you have done it now." Then the father turned to Lorenzo Spain and grasped his hand. "Thanks, brother, for bringing our girl home. We just about died of fright."

"I hear you," Pop told him. "I got one too. I know what you're going through. It's like having a wild animal in the house. Never know what they're gonna do next."

The second stop was at the Edson house, where Trudy Edson had just arrived home to find all the messages on her answering machine. She rushed out and cried, "What is going on?"

Pop stepped out of the Civic. "Lady, your daughter here and two other kids went joyriding with a dopehead. Coulda been killed. You and your husband, you better cut back on your busy lives, you hear what I'm saying? You got a loose cannon here."

"Athena!" her mother gasped.

"Oh Mom," Athena protested, "it wasn't that bad."

Finally, Pop, Jaris, and Chelsea headed home.

"I'm really sorry," Chelsea said again. "This guy said we'd just go for a spin around the school in this Mercedes. Keisha thought it'd be fun just to ride in one for a few minutes. We had no idea . . . "

"Yeah, it was fun all right," Pop agreed. "And there was more exciting stuff ahead. You almost got to ride in a hearse. You know what a hearse is, little girl? That's where they put dead people. When you hit something at a hundred miles an hour, you're either dead or you wish you were dead."

They pulled into the Spain driveway and Mom came rushing out. As soon as Chelsea got out of the car, Mom hugged her. "Oh baby, I was so scared. I thought I'd never see you alive again. I never want to go through anything like that again!"

Pop reached Chelsea and he hugged her too. "I sweat blood, little girl," he told her. "When Inessa said you sped off in a creepy car with two dopeheads, I didn't want to live no more. I couldn't deal with burying you, kid."

Pop then pushed off Chelsea to arm's length. He looked into her eyes and said in a harsh voice, "Girl, you are grounded. You are so grounded you gonna forget what freedom is. No more riding your bike or walkin' to school." Chelsea began to cry a little. Pop continued. "Me or your mom or Jaris gonna pick you up from school and take you there. You ain't visiting at no friend's house. You ain't hanging out anywhere. If you wanna see somebody, they're coming to this house and visiting you. You turned wild, girl, and we ain't taking no more chances. Y'hear what I'm saying?"

Chelsea ran into the house and flung herself on the bed in her room. She grasped the biggest teddy bear she had and hugged it tightly. She cried in loud sobs. She wasn't crying because she thought her punishment was unjust. She was crying because her parents didn't trust her anymore. She was crying because she was losing so much freedom she had gained since becoming a teenager. She was crying because she knew she had failed them all—and herself.

This time Mom didn't argue with Pop about his discipline. The police called to tell them that Cory Yates had been arrested for driving under the influence of drugs and alcohol. Brandon was also taken down to juvenile hall with a high level of drugs and alcohol in his system as well. "Good!" Pop said with satisfaction. "Those bum parents are letting their kids run wild. When the cops do a little digging, they'll probably find out the brother is a drug dealer up in LA. How else does a guy his age afford a Mercedes?"

"And Chelsea got in that car," Mom sighed. "Lorenzo, how does that happen?"

Pop took a deep breath and spoke. "You tell me, babe. We've done our best. We love the kids with all our heart. Chelsea knows that. But then there's the temptation to take a risk and she goes for it. The immature friends help make the bad decision. But now it's gonna be different. We're gonna watch that little wildflower until she's got enough sense to handle herself better."

Jaris went into his sister's room about an hour later. She had stopped crying and she was leaning on her teddy bear. She looked about ten years old.

"Chili pepper, how you doing?" Jaris asked.

Chelsea shrugged. "I blew it,," she groaned, "Jaris. I blew everything. I swore to you that I'd never be with Brandon again after what happened at that party. Then I climb in his brother's car and . . . what was I thinking?"

"Yeah," Jaris said.

"Jaris, you're so perfect," Chelsea told him. "How come you're so perfect?"

"I'm not," Jaris protested. "I've screwed up too, chili pepper. I've done stupid things.

They say what doesn't kill you makes you stronger, and this'll make you stronger. It didn't kill you, but it came close. But at least you had the smarts to get out of the car first chance you got and not ride back with those creeps.".

"Oh Jaris," Chelsea sighed, "I bet it was going through Mom and Pop's mind that maybe Grandma Jessie is right, that I should be sent to some old boarding school. Maybe I'd be better off locked away in Santa Barbara."

Jaris shook his head. "No, chili pepper, that's a no-brainer. They love you too much for that."

"I love them too, Jaris," Chelsea said. "And I love you too. You know, during that horrible ride, Cory Yates almost hit another car head-on when he was passing a slow moving car. And I had this horrible vision. I was in a casket at the Holiness Awakening Church, and Mom and Pop and you were standing around my casket crying. And I felt so bad I'd done that to you guys."

"You made it, sis," Jaris assured her, kissing the top of his sister's head. "You made it, chili pepper."

The next day, the word was out at Tubman High. Inessa Weaver's sister, Cassie, was a junior at Tubman. Jaris didn't know Cassie Weaver well. But she was telling everyone what those three foolish girls at Anderson Middle School did. Cassie was regaling her friends and bystanders about how her smart little sister not only refused to go along in the Mercedes, but also alerted everyone about what happened.

"Inessa is nobody's fool," Cassie bragged. "But those other girls, what airheads! They pile in this car with a druggie at the wheel."

Among those listening to the story were Marko Lane and his girlfriend, Jasmine. They listened to Cassie telling all the details, and then they walked on to Mr. Pippin's English class. Along the way they ran into Jaris.

"Hey Jaris," Marko called, "I hear your little sister's running with drug addicts and going for wild rides in a big Mercedes, a shiny silver Mercedes."

"She made one stupid mistake," Jaris snapped. "She got in the car with two friends and they're all sorry."

"Yeah?" Marko retorted. "I'm hearing on the grapevine that your whole family is fallin' apart, man." Marko looked gleeful. Jaris Spain had been an annoyance to Marko for a long time. Marko had wanted to date Sereeta, but she chose Jaris instead. Jaris made better grades than Marko, and he was better liked all around school. And Marko resented that Jaris's friends were on the track team with Marko and that they often outshone him. Often in class, Jaris made Marko look like a fool. Now it pleased Marko to think there was trouble in that perfect Spain family.

"You're crazy," Jaris said. "My family is fine."

"I'm thinking you got money problems," Marko guessed, fishing for more information. "My mom's cousin works at the bank. And your old man was in there the other day talking about a loan. You guys goin' under or something? Too many credit cards?"

"Know what, Marko?" Jaris snapped. "It's none of your business."

Jasmine laughed. "That means it's true, dude," Marko laughed. Marko felt like he had hit a sore spot. "You goin' down, dude."

Jaris had not shared the fact that his father wanted to buy Jackson's garage with anybody but his closest friends. He certainly wouldn't share his family's affairs with Marko. Friends like Sami Archer, Trevor Jenkins, Alonee Lennox, and, of course, Sereeta knew. "Think what you want," Jaris blew him off.

"And your sister," Jasmine chimed in, "pretty soon she gonna be like that Bethany Walsh who hung with B.J. She's only fourteen and already she's hanging with dopers."

"But I gotta say this," Marko added, with an evil smirk on his face, "Chelsea is hot. That girl is *hot*. I seen her in your front yard the other day with her tiny straps and her short-shorts. And I thought this is one hot little chick."

There was nobody around but the three of them at the corner of the English building. Just Jaris, Marko, and Jasmine. Jaris turned sharply and grabbed Marko's shirtfront, ramming him against the stucco wall. He held the shirtfront so tight that Marko gasped for air. "Don't you talk about my sister with your dirty mouth, Lane," he growled,. "Don't you trash her, you hear me?"

"Back off!" Jasmine warned. "You're strangling him."

"I'm warning you, man," Jaris snarled. "Chelsea is off limits for your trash talk, understand?" Jaris let Marko go then, just as Mr. Pippin appeared, carrying his battered briefcase. Mr. Pippin took a quick look at Marko Lane, gasping for air. He glanced at Jaris, seeing the hatred in the boy's face. Mr. Pippin knew something bad had just happened. Marko's eyes were wild. His shirt was askew. Mr. Pippin knew that some sort of altercation had just taken place, but Mr. Pippin made no inquiry. He didn't know what happened, and he didn't want to know. If he knew, he would have to get involved. So Mr. Pippin ignored what he saw and hurried into his classroom, grateful to have escaped whatever happened.

Jaris went into the classroom, leaving Marko leaning against the wall and Jasmine quietly scolding him, probably for calling any other girl "hot."

Jaris struggled to concentrate on English. He was worried about the loan his father wanted to take out. He was worried that at the last minute Mom would refuse to cosign. He was worried about Chelsea too. She was getting rebellious, and now with the new restrictions, would she rebel totally? Where would that behavior lead? Would there be more arguments between Mom and Pop?

Jaris feared Chelsea would run away, as some kids do. Jaris's friend, Trevor Jenkins, had had a girlfriend—Vanessa Allen. She had run away from her family when she was fifteen. Her life went all downhill from there. She hadn't found her way back, and maybe never would.

Jaris hoped his parents, especially Pop, had the wisdom not to crack down so hard on Chelsea that she would give up hope. Jaris hoped they wouldn't stifle her. Pop had called her a wildflower, and wildflowers are very fragile. If you held one tightly in your hand, it wilted and shriveled up. You had to give even a wildflower a little room to breathe.

Two days later, as Jaris was driving Chelsea home from Anderson, she asked her brother for advice. "Jaris, Heston Crawford and I are working on a science project at school. His family is kinda poor and they don't have a computer. He'd like to come over and work with me on my computer. You think that'd be okay?"

Jaris hesitated. Pop already had a run-in with Heston when he sat on the curb with Chelsea. Pop accused Heston of drooling over Chelsea in her skimpy outfit.

"I don't know, chili pepper," Jaris replied. "Pop's home, so you could ask him."

"Oh Jaris, he's gonna say no!" Chelsea protested. "I need to study with Heston. Heston is kind of a geek, but he's such a genius in science. We got this really complicated project and I want an A. . . . Uh, Jaris, would *you* ask Pop for me?"

"Uh . . . yeah, sure," Jaris agreed. He didn't want to tangle with Pop either, especially with the Jackson deal hanging. Every night he heard his parents going back and forth about it. Mom kept stressing her misgivings. Pop kept repeating that this was his last chance to score. Jaris thought the outcome could go either way, and Pop was generally in a bad mood. What happened with Chelsea in the Mercedes made him even darker.

Chelsea hurried to her room, leaving Jaris to confront his father in the kitchen.

"Mmm, smells good, Pop," Jaris commented.

"What does?" Pop asked in an annoyed voice. "I ain't even started yet."

Jaris felt like a fool. He'd blown it already.

"I'm trying to decide if I should make chicken manicotti or scallops in cream sauce," Pop thought out loud. Then he spoke to Jaris. "Your mom likes scallops. I'm trying to butter her up, you know. I'm trying to do everything right to get on her good side, so she comes with me and signs the second mortgage. I guess I better go with the scallops."

"Uh Pop," Jaris began, "you know Chelsea has this tough science class and she's hoping to make an A. The kids, they got partners in their projects, and she's partners with this kid who's really smart in science. Problem is, this other kid's family is poor and they don't have a computer. So would it be okay if they worked on Chelsea's computer in her room?"

"Sure," Pop consented, melting margarine in the skillet to cook onions and then adding the scallops. "The other girl can come over anytime, Jaris. I got no objection to that."

"Well," Jaris went on. "It's a guy. It's Heston Crawford. Uh . . . he's good in science, and they need to do research, him and Chelsea. So, you know, she can maybe earn an A. He was wondering if he could come over this afternoon and work with Chelsea."

"I know that kid," Pop remarked. "He was with Chelsea the other day, plunked himself down on the curb. And she was there in those itty-bitty clothes."

"Pop," Jaris said, "Chelsea asked me to ask you . . . you know, for permission." Just looking at Pop standing there with the smoking skillet was scary.

Pop stirred in the scallops. Then he mixed wine and cornstarch, and he stirred that into the scallops. Next he added the whipping cream. "Your mom will go crazy for this," he said. "Put her in a real good mood." He stopped then and spoke to Jaris. "He can come over. The Crawford kid can come over. I kinda like him. He's got respect."

Jaris hurried to Chelsea's room. "It's okay, chili pepper. Pop said Heston can come over."

"Thanks, Jaris!" Chelsea said, calling Heston quickly.

CHAPTER TEN

In about ten minutes, Heston Crawford biked up. He saw Mr. Spain and he said, "Afternoon sir. Me and Chelsea are doing this project on the solar system. Our teacher, she's real particular, so we gotta get the newest stuff off the Internet. They're coming up with new discoveries every day, you know."

"I bet they are," Pop replied. "Good luck. We want to get that old solar system straight. Everything on earth is going to Hades in a handbasket. But we gotta figure out what those black holes are all about."

"Yes sir," Heston responded, as if he hadn't heard the sarcasm in Pop's voice.

Mom came home in a bad mood. Jaris thought that not even the scallops and cream sauce could help. "Greg and I have decided which teachers will go if the budget mess isn't resolved," she explained. "Oh, we were so torn. It'll be that enthusiastic second-grade teacher and the young man who's so good teaching math."

"Maybe the idiots in the capitol will come up with a budget," Pop suggested.

"I don't know where all this is going, Lorenzo," Mom sighed. "You'd think the last thing to be cut would be education. Our nation is already behind other countries in math and science, and now we're cutting budgets even more. I mean, how soon will it be before even teachers with experience will be sent packing? *Teachers like me*!"

"Oh, they'd never can you, Monie. You're the top of the line," Pop assured her.

"Don't be too sure," Mom replied in a grumpy voice.

Jaris was afraid Mom was making the situation sound even more dire than it was.

He thought maybe she was making a last-ditch effort to convince Pop that even her job might be in jeopardy. Then wouldn't it be utter folly to put a new mortgage on the house and take a risky leap in starting a business? As long as Mom's job was secure, the family would at least have her paycheck to fall back on. Now she was reminding Pop that maybe even that safety net had holes in it.

Mom heard Heston talking in Chelsea's room. "Who's that?" she asked.

"Little guy named Heston Crawford," Pop answered. "He and Chelsea working on a science project. He's okay. I gave him a hard time the other day when he was sitting on the curb with Chelsea, but he was polite. I can see he's a good kid. The family is up against it, so they don't have a computer. They're using Chelsea's."

"A lot of families are hard up," Mom replied, seizing every opportunity to make her point. "Times aren't good."

"Yeah, but even in bad times, there's opportunity, babe," Pop objected. "Sometimes the best opportunities come in bad times."

Jaris could see his parents dancing around the issue, like fencers jabbing with their swords. Neither of them wanted to come right out and argue.

On his way out, Heston stopped in the kitchen. "We got a lot done," he reported. "Thanks for letting me come over."

"Sure Heston," Pop responded, "anytime."

"Your daughter is very smart," Heston added. "It's nice working with her."

Mom smiled and said, "That's nice of you to say."

When Heston was gone, Mom commented, "He *is* sweet."

"Yeah," Pop agreed. "He knows how to butter the bread. With all the sassy-mouthed punks around, it's refreshing to meet a kid like him."

The family sat down to dinner.

"These scallops are wonderful," Mom remarked. Then she started talking about all the bad economic news on the television. Pop just sat there with a faraway look in his eyes. He was eighteen years old again, on the brink of an athletic scholarship. He was going to college. He would major in science and be somebody. The future was bright with promise. Then came the sports injury and the end of his dream. Now he'd caught hold of a new dream. It filled his mind. He thought about it before he went to bed at night and first thing when he got up in the morning.

Pop never went back to his high school reunions. He didn't want to face his old friends and admit to them that the dream died and that he was only a mechanic. But he thought perhaps in a year or two he would go to a high school reunion. And he'd tell everybody about his new business, his flourishing auto care business. He would bring pictures of the shop. It would be freshly painted with his name in bold letters.

CHAPTER TEN

The Spain's appointment with the loan officer at the bank was on Friday. On Thursday night, Jaris heard his parents discussing the matter. Mom was still torn by fears. Pop was still determined. They weren't arguing anymore. They were just talking. But there was terror in Mom's voice, and there was desperation in Pop's voice. His dream hung by a thread, and his wife's trembling hands held scissors.

Jaris went to school on Friday morning, still very unsure about how things would turn out. When he and his friends gathered for lunch under the eucalyptus trees, everybody was there. They all knew Jaris wanted his father to get the loan and the garage. They all knew how much it meant to Jaris that his father would finally have something to be proud of.

"I think the news'll be good," Sereeta declared. "I just have a feeling." Sereeta was still glowing from her trip to San Francisco with her mother. She thought if a miracle like that could happen, then surely Lorenzo Spain's dream could come true too.

"Sometimes," Sereeta continued, "the sky is so dark that you think you'll never see the sun again. Then it breaks through, and the sun is brighter than you have ever seen it before."

"Yeah," Alonee agreed. "We've all had times like that when things were kinda dark, but then it's good again."

Trevor looked sad for a moment. He was thinking about his relationship with Vanessa Allen and how it was over. And a shy girl in his science class had mustered up the courage to talk to him. Trevor thought he might ask her out. Maybe someday soon she would join him and his friends for lunch under the eucalyptus trees.

"Yeah," Oliver Randall added. "You know, when I first came to Tubman, I didn't have any friends. You guys reached out to me, and now I feel like I've been going here since ninth grade. Alonee called it 'the posse,' and it's a great bunch. It's not the in-group and it's not the out-group. . . . It's just friends."

Kevin Walker nodded. "Same with me. I blew in from Texas scared out of my wits. I was a loner. But when I was in the pits, you guys were there, pulling me through."

Jaris lay back on the grass and watched the cirrus clouds sail by. A seagull from nowhere glided overhead. He laughed a little. "Hey Derrick," he chuckled, "do you remember that time the seagull pooped on Marko's head?"

Derrick laughed too. "That was a smart seagull, bro," he said.

"I wonder if seagulls ever worry about anything?" Jaris asked. "They fly around with such a peaceful look."

Everybody laughed.

"They're probably kinda dumb," Derrick responded, "and they don't think about much—like me."

Destini poked Derrick and told him, "You're not dumb, babe, so quit saying that."

"How can we know for sure if seagulls think or not?" Oliver wondered. "I mean, who's ever asked a seagull whether they worry if there'll be enough fish for them to eat or if a storm's coming up."

"When I was little," Carissa, Kevin's girlfriend, said, "I read a story about all the animals and birds being able to talk on one day—on Christmas. And everybody gathered to hear what they had to say. That would be nice, I think."

Sereeta watched the seagull slowly disappear in the blue sky. "Birds are the only animals I have ever envied," she said. "I mean, I never thought it must be great to be an antelope or a cheetah. But birds—wow!—that must be wonderful, to just fly wherever you want to go. Not sitting in a seat on a plane, but really to fly."

Sami Archer giggled. "I feel sorry for the little furry things that are stuck on the ground. The rabbits and the chipmunks. They gotta really scratch to make a livin'. Y'hear what I'm sayin'? Especially the ones who live in the city, where their homes are all vanishin' 'cause we're buildin' everywhere. Like when we don't get no rain, I worry about the rabbits findin' enough greens to eat."

"They're all in my mother's garden," Jaris declared. "Every year Mom plans to feed us all our veggies from her garden. She plants tomatoes, peppers, lettuce, everything. And at night the bunnies come out and eat everything in sight. Those rabbits got our address, I'm telling you. Mom gets so upset, but Pop just laughs. He'll go 'Peter Rabbit come to call again.' "

Jaris looked at his watch. He often got pains in his stomach when he was nervous. Right now he felt big-time pains. The appointment at the bank was at one thirty. That was in an hour and a half. Mom was supposed to take time off from her work to meet Pop at the bank. A substitute teacher would fill in with Mom's lesson plans. That was the plan anyway. Jaris didn't know if it would happen like that or not.

Jaris couldn't imagine what it would be like tonight at the house if the deal fell through, if Pop's dream was officially over. It was almost too sad to imagine. Yet Jaris couldn't be angry with his mother if she ended up refusing to sign. She couldn't help being afraid for the family's security.

The plan was for Pop to pick up the cashier's check for the amount of the loan and take it directly to Mr. Jackson. By this afternoon, the garage would belong to Pop. Unless Mom didn't sign. Then, Jackson said, he had two other buyers who were willing and eager to buy the place.

Jaris struggled through his afternoon classes. He kept dragging his mind back to the subjects at hand. He kept trying to convince himself that the Kennedy administration, which they were studying in Ms. McDowell's class, was more important than his family's fate. Most of the time he failed.

Jaris had a cell phone, but he didn't want to call to find out what happened. He didn't want his parents to call him either. Whatever happened, he didn't want to hear about it over the phone.

After classes at Tubman, Jaris and Sereeta got into Jaris's Honda and headed for Anderson Middle School to pick up Chelsea. Jaris had told Sereeta more than he told his other friends. He shared with her how much this garage deal meant to his father.

"It's gonna break him if it doesn't go down." Jaris was fretting as they left Tubman.

"I think it'll be okay, Jaris," Sereeta assured him. She reached over and squeezed Jaris's hand.

They picked up Chelsea and then drove toward Jackson's garage. If the news was good, Jaris wanted Sereeta and Chelsea to be there with him. If the news was bad, he needed them even more.

"I'm so scared," Chelsea admitted. "Poor Pop . . . I mean . . ." She never finished the sentence.

The drive to Jackson's garage was only a couple of miles. Jaris gripped the steering wheel tightly to keep his hands from shaking. Sereeta ran her soft hand against his cheek. They were almost there.

They turned the corner. As they drove up, there were cars at Jackson's garage, as usual. As usual, Pop was wearing his blue uniform, his "monkey suit" as he called it. And, as usual, he was leaning over an engine.

Then they saw the other two men. They were from a sign company. They were mounting ladders toward the front of the garage. They had already painted out the name Jackson.

"Look!" Sereeta said in a hushed voice. "They're painting an 'S' on the sign . . . "

Chelsea let out a scream. "And a 'P'!" she cried.

Pop saw them then. He came walking over. "Hey kids, hey Sereeta. I'm all filthy with grease and stuff, so don't—" he said.

But they came at him anyway, all three of them, hugging him in spite of the grease and the grime. The brown gunk was all over them, and they didn't care. They were screaming, laughing, and jumping up and down.

Mom came around the corner. She had started the day wearing a pretty pink blouse. It too was covered with grease because she had hugged him first. Mom grinned and plucked at a grease stain. "Don't worry," she said, "it'll all come out in the wash."

The four of them stood there, laughing and crying and hugging one another. They knew that, whatever happened—whatever they kept and whatever they lost—they would always have their love for one another. Nothing could ever take that away from them.

Jaris knew that and he felt that. And when he saw Pop sweep up Chelsea in his powerful arms, Jaris could see that their little wildflower knew it and felt it too.